When Laura Trevillick is goaded into w
house, she never dreams that it will
building. And when she does get inside
doors click shut? Like Alice in Wonderland, Laura frighteningly
finds herself in a time and place far removed from her quiet
Cornish village and it is only after a series of extraordinary and
dangerous adventures that she <u>thinks</u> she finds herself back home
again. But the house with the locked door has other ideas and at
the end the way is open to further journeys into the unknown.

An adventure series for all children aged 9 - 15

This book is for Rachel and Kerensa

The Locked Door
Book 1: Enter Laura

Harvey Kurzfield

Published in 2009 by New Generation Publishing

First Edition

Published by New Generation Publishing

Prologue

The house has been part of this and many other universes for thousands of years. It does not know how it came into existence, nor, precisely, its purpose. It can only admit one individual per universe. This might, at first, seem limiting, but, given the number of universes, both parallel and co-existing in time and space, the opportunities are limitless.

The house has a consciousness that is unique and a predisposition towards its own moral code, the benefits of which are not always apparent to those allowed inside.

The house is not exactly a 'law unto itself', but nor does it always obey perceived laws of physics. As such, any person, human or otherwise, that enters, does so at their own risk. Having said that, entry is by invitation only – whether or not such an invitation is desired or requested.

There is no indication of danger. To the unsuspecting visitor all might seem normal; whatever that is.
He or she soon finds out that all is very far from 'normal' particularly when that house has a locked door......

Chapter 1

"Coward! Coward! Coward!"

The voices chanted mercilessly. Not that they were deliberately cruel. It was just a game. Laura, who stood in the middle, surrounded by a circle of similarly aged children from the village, braced her shoulders defiantly. Normally, she would not have allowed herself to be goaded into taking any action which she felt she might later regret. On this occasion, however, she wanted to accept the challenge. There was something about the old house which reached out to her. It had been empty for many years. The owner, it was believed, lived abroad, and had never been seen. Children, postmen, cats, dogs, burglars and salesmen and women generally avoided the place, instinctively. Consequently it had earned itself a reputation. Laura had, as usual, been walking through the village on her own, soaking up the sights and sounds and transferring them into her sketch book. She had come across this group during the course of her walk and they had followed her demanding to look at her sketches. Laura had stubbornly refused. Her sketches, she declared, were private, like a diary – her secret. The wheedling and threatening had been kept up for some distance. Then they had all found themselves in front of the house. Here they had stopped.

"I bet it's haunted," said May.

That had been the start of everything. As the outsider, the newest arrival in the village, Laura had become the hub at which the established children chipped.

"We've all been in there," lied John

"Yeah!" chorused his friends.

"If you wanna be one of us you've got to go in," said Beth.

At first, Laura had refused. It was silly and anyway she would be trespassing. Besides, it was all locked up. She had turned to continue her walk. That's when the chanting had started – coward, coward, coward.

"Alright!" She yelled.

The chanting stopped and the children waited expectantly. Holding her head high, Laura walked confidently through the gate and down the garden path. On either side she could see a profusion of wild, but gloriously coloured flowers. These had not been visible from the road outside. Laura looked back over her shoulder.

"Go on," they called.

She lifted her shoulders and continued, quite sure that the front door would be locked and that when she failed to find a way in would be able to return, honour satisfied. The door grew larger as Laura approached. It was constructed from thick, dark wood and looked quite ancient. She had expected it to have peeling paint or varnish, but, instead, it appeared to be in near perfect condition. Laura stretched her hand towards the octagonal door knob…. but before her hand reached it there was a sharp little click and the door opened. Laura peered round and stared inside. There was a hall and at the far end a wide staircase. She turned again to look at the group of children. They seemed a long way away. Stranger still, they were talking and playing and no longer paying her any attention.

"They might at least have kept watching….," thought Laura.

With an air of defiance she turned again and walked briskly into the hall. There was a definite contrast between the chill of the indoors and the warmth of the late summer sunshine outside. Behind her, the door quietly closed.

"Hello," Laura called. Silence greeted her. There were closed doors leading off the hall. Somehow the stairs were the most promising prospect. After all, she could run up one flight, turn, and run back down again. Clutching her sketchbook tightly, Laura scampered up the steps, her feet making no sound on the soft, luxurious carpet, from which rose not the slightest trace of dust.

She reached the first landing and came to a window. There was the most splendid view across the fields. Quickly, Laura opened her sketch book and began to draw trees, fields, animals – everything she could see. When she turned at last, she glanced down the stairs and realised that the front door was closed. When had that happened? She wondered for a moment whether one of the children had raced down the pathway and shut her in. Well, they would soon realise that she would not be so easily frightened. She looked at her surroundings. The staircase branched off in two directions, but from where she stood she could see that they both came out onto an open gallery.

'If I go up one way, rather than another, will I find myself in a different place, like Alice?' Laura smiled at her whimsical notion; this was, after all, the twenty first century. Taking a deep breath, she closed her sketch book and walked gracefully up the right-hand staircase. She expected to see portraits of lords and ladies, but the walls were simply papered in a pleasantly decorative manner. Having reached the top, she crossed the landing, ran down the left-hand staircase, across the landing and back up the way she had first come. Nothing happened. She smiled ruefully.

In front of her the landing seemed to be a room to itself, with chairs, a sofa and several chests. On one wall there was an ornate, full length mirror. Laura crossed to it and looked at her reflection. She saw her own self staring back, a little self-consciously; a tall girl, bright blue eyes in a round, pale face topped by blonde, slightly spiky hair. Laura smiled at her herself. Her reflection, however, remained unsmiling. She turned away quickly then and saw that directly facing her was a door. She walked forward and was not too surprised when the door clicked open to reveal a pleasant room with soft-cushioned chairs and comfortable furnishings. She walked straight in and went immediately to the window overlooking the front garden. To her disappointment the children were no longer by the front gate.

With a sense of being let down, she turned and walked back to the door. It was shut. She knew she had left it open just as she knew that the reflection in the mirror should have smiled back at her. Laura stretched out her hand expecting the door to open of its own accord. Nothing happened. Tutting to herself, she grasped the handle and tried to turn it. It did not move. She tried again. She tried turning it the other way: she tried pulling it. She tried kicking the door. She even screamed at the door! Just as before, nothing happened. The door was well and truly locked.

Chapter 2

Angrily, Laura kicked at the door once more. There was the faintest of sounds – like a sigh. A feeling of anxiety swept over Laura as she realised how dark the room now seemed; in fact, the only light was emanating from a small bulb hanging from the centre of the ceiling.

"I'll climb out the window," thought Laura.

She turned and gasped. Where there had been two large windows was now only a plain wall with no openings whatsoever. Laura stamped her foot and gave a scream of frustration and fear. There was a chuckle, somehow, from the room itself. A voice said, "Welcome, Laura."

Then the light went out.

Laura remained standing completely still. That she was very, very frightened was unmistakeable. But she had reserves of courage which had stood her in good stead in many encounters with other children, adults, even unfriendly adults. So she did not panic – yet. There was certainly something wrong in this situation, something way out of the ordinary. She dismissed the idea that the children outside had rigged this specially for her. This was far too sophisticated for a group of Cornish schoolchildren. She waited, listening. There was no sound, no murmurs, no more chuckling. She had no sense of any other presence except her own. The darkness was almost peaceful; and then she recalled the voice that had said 'Welcome Laura.' There had been no hint of malice or menace. Perhaps the welcome was genuine. Slowly Laura sank to the floor, clutching her precious sketchbook close to her chest. There was no sense of oppression, but she was beginning to feel completely drained of energy. Without thinking too much about anything at all, Laura lay on the ground, pleasantly surprised to find the floor covering quite warm and comforting. Quite soon she was fast asleep.

Which was just exactly what the house had been waiting for.

Chapter 3

Some time later Laura woke up. Her sketch book lay open on the floor.

'I didn't leave it like that,' she thought, then realised with genuine surprise and delight that the room was light again, indeed, bright with daylight. She turned and there was the door she had come through – open! With a cry of relief Laura snatched up her sketchbook and raced towards the door, half expecting it to slam in her face. But it didn't. As she ran down the stairs it felt almost as if she was air assisted; and was that a voice again? What was it saying? She paused for a second and could just make out the words: 'Have a nice day, Laura. Be careful. And come back soon.'

'Ha!' thought Laura. 'Not if I can help it!'

She ran across the lower hall and out through the front door, also wide open for her, down the garden and through the gate. Then stopped in utter amazement. The scene which now confronted her was one with which she was entirely unfamiliar. The Cornish village which she called 'home' was just not there any longer. What was 'there' was a scene, which, to her young eyes, seemed like a concreted yard. Laura rubbed her eyes; an instinctive reaction. She thought that she must still be dreaming.

- 'I'll have to go back inside,'- she decided and turned with the reluctant intention of retracing her steps. The shock of what she saw held her rooted to the spot. The house was no longer there. Instead, it had been replaced by a tall structure with what looked like tinted glass all over. She saw this through a tall, black, wrought-iron gate. On the seemingly endless wall around the property was a sign, with very plain print on a white background – 'Research and Development Institute' – was all it gave away. What use was that to Laura? She backed away from the gate, shuddering. Then, in a kind of despairing way, turned and ran as fast as she could, and then fell heavily as the ground beneath her feet moved. She moved awkwardly away from what she could now see was a moving part of the walkway on which she had been running. She rubbed her sore arm, which still clutched her sketch book – her only link with her own reality. As she sat there she saw something in the distance approaching at an alarming speed. The 'something' gradually became an object like a train, only there were no rails as such; just a shiny oval dip in the concrete surface. There was a solitary 'hoot' as the 'train' sped past her, a single coach about 30 metres long. She tried to see if there were passengers but the windows were tinted. She watched the train for a while, then stood up as she realised that some way off it had come to a halt and people were getting down. With a growing sense of excitement Laura walked swiftly towards the place where the train had halted, for surely it meant that somewhere up ahead there was a station?

While she was walking Laura became aware that it was uncomfortably hot and that her pale skin was tingling. Placing her sketch book over her head to try and prevent sunburn she continued walking, anxious now to find somewhere to shelter. Unfortunately the 'station' was nothing more than a short stopping place. There was no platform as such, no ticket office, no billboards, no buildings, no kiosks and definitely no people to collect or dispense tickets. Her eyes, however, were becoming more accustomed to the variations in the patterns on the concrete ground and she could just make out a strip that seemed to be flowing; and as she concentrated she could make out, along the strip, the people who had, only a short time ago, got off the train. They seemed very small and very distant. Carefully, remembering how easily she had fallen, she made her way towards the strip. As Laura came closer she could see that it was quite wide, rather like an airport strip at Heathrow; she had been there quite a few times with her parents so was familiar with such things. The strip was moving at a fairly swift space, but, even so, she felt confident that she could judge the speed by running alongside it and then skip on to it reasonably safely. Taking a deep breath she ran alongside the moving strip and then put her plan into action. It worked, with only a slight stumble on landing. Laura took some more deep breaths to control the rate at which her heart was beating. As she grew calmer she could see that the strip was taking her closer and closer towards a huge area, dominated by enormous skyscrapers. Looking behind her she was surprised to see water close by. Lots of water. How was that possible?

The buildings seemed to grow even taller as she sped now towards them. Gradually Laura realised that she was approaching what appeared to be a walled town. Signs by the side of the moving pathway became activated and she read:
'You are now entering the City State of Bodmin.' Further on another sign revealed the message: 'Please come in Peace and you will be treated well.' Finally,

'Please make sure you have your food vouchers.' Laura raised her eyebrows. What were food vouchers and what happened if you did not have any? Laura had recently completed a project on the Second World War and so she knew something about food rationing in Britain in the years immediately following the war. She wondered if that was what was meant by 'food vouchers'. She realised that she was still in Cornwall because only a short time ago she had driven through Bodmin. It had never looked like this though and had certainly not been known as a 'city state'.

At last she was nearing Bodmin itself. The moving path looked as if it just disappeared into a wall, but as she drew closer, a section of the wall automatically slid open for her and she passed through. She felt a tingling sensation on her body and wondered if, perhaps, she'd been scanned in some way. The road continued to move and she was able to look at the tall structures which surrounded her on either side. They were all glass and concrete but she was unable to see into any building as all the glass, if that's what it was, had been tinted. All she saw were her own reflections passing in bewilderment. There were no shops, no pedestrians, no vehicles, no grass, no weeds, no dogs – in short, the whole place looked deserted. Staring ahead she realised that there was a break in the pattern. The moving walkway was slowing down and it looked as if she was heading for some kind of piazza, or at least an open space of some sort. Then she saw another screen. She could make out the words 'Getting Around Bodmin', so she hopped off the pathway with no difficulty and carefully walked towards the screen. The display changed as she drew nearer. 'Welcome to the City State of Bodmin. You are here.' A map appeared on the screen with a red arrow pointing to a small spot in the centre of the map. Dotted around her position were the names of various buildings – Museum of Fine Art; Recreation Centre; Exercise Centre; Town Hall; Police Station. Laura drew in her breath. A police station! That ought to be the place where she went first. Surely the police would be able to help her?

She touched the part of the screen that said 'Police Station' and the screen came up with 'Follow the blue spots. They will lead you to your destination.' Laura looked down. Leading from the screen was indeed a line of blue spots. "Thanks," she said and a spoken message immediately replied 'You are welcome.' Laura wondered where the voice had come from but began to follow the spots. They led straight across the piazza to a building less tall than many others she had seen. The only indication that this was a police station was the flashing blue light above the entrance. Laura realised her heart was pounding so she waited for a short while to calm down. Looking around she still could not make out any signs of movement or any sounds. Everything in the city state of Bodmin seemed silent and still. By now she was so hot that she had to find a shady area in which to cool down.

She was ready to mount the steps and did so speculating on how she would get in and who she would meet and whether the doors would be locked, but after passing through another light scan the doors at the top slid open, noiselessly. Laura hadn't known what to expect, but in her wildest imaginings she had not expected a wall of telephones. She looked around for an enquiry desk. No luck – just phones. She walked to the closest phone. There were four numbered buttons. She lifted the receiver to her ear.

"Hello, welcome," said a soft, slightly synthetic female voice. "If you wish to report a crime, please press button 1. If you wish to claim lost or stolen property please press button 2. If you have been called in for an interview, please press button 3. For all other enquiries, please press button 4."

Laura took a deep breath and pressed button 4 as this was, clearly, her only option. Immediately a reassuringly deep, male voice answered. "Hello, how can I help you?" Laura thought quickly. "I'm lost," she said. There was a pause. "How do you mean, lost?"

"Lost, you know, I haven't the faintest idea where I am."

"OK, someone will come out to speak to you. Put the phone on the hook and wait in the circled area."

The line went dead. Laura looked at the floor then moved into a blue flashing circle in the centre of the waiting area. A camera lens appeared above the bank of phones. It looked at her and slowly moved up and down. Obviously, no chances were taken in this police station. After a while a section of wall slid aside and a man in a uniform stood there waiting. Laura did not recognise the uniform. It looked more military than police-like.

"Come this way young lady." He beckoned to her. She did not move. "Come on, this way, no need to look so worried, I'm not going to eat you."

The remark was so ordinary and unremarkable that Laura suddenly lost her fear and stepped forward. The door through which she passed slid back in to place. Laura wondered if it would lock itself behind her.

The man remained standing. He saw Laura's worried face.

"It's ok, we're just going down."

"Down? Down where?"

"Way down below where it's much cooler and much safer for you. I hope you haven't been out there too long."

Laura was wondering what he meant when a very slight vibration suggested they were stopping.

"Here we are," said her new companion, disappearing through a panel which slid open.

Chapter 4

The uniformed man was walking along a corridor. Laura followed, quickening her pace to match the lengthy stride of her guide.

"Excuse me," she called. "Where are we going?"

"Interview room," was all the reply she got.

They arrived at a dead end. The wall in front of them slid aside and they entered an empty office space.

"Still with me then?"

Laura, who had paused for a good look round, quickly followed her guide again. They came to a door marked 'Interview Room 2'.

"In here then," said the uniform. "Come on, smile, it'll soon be sorted out."

Laura wasn't so sure. Even with all this advanced technology it seemed likely that her predicament would not be so easy to solve.

The room they now entered surprised her. She had watched a few detective programmes on television and expected to find herself in an austere, grim, cell-like cubby hole. Instead, the floor was carpeted and there were four comfortable looking seats suspended from the ceiling. A young woman, also in uniform, stood up from one of the chairs and came forward to greet Laura.

"Hullo there," she said welcomingly. "Come and sit down."

She showed Laura to one of the chairs and Laura, carefully, sat down. The seat was steady and did not rock as she slipped into it. It was very comfortable, almost seeming to mould itself to fit her slim body.

"Now is there anything we can get you? Would you like a drink or something to eat?"

Laura asked for a drink.

"Right Madam, I shall see to it at once!" said her escort.

"Thanks Doug, you're a real gentleman." The officer who said this sat down facing Laura and smiled reassuringly.

"My name's Detective Flick, Samantha Flick; but you can call me Sam."

Laura's shoulders suddenly relaxed; she grimaced as the release in tension made her realise how stiff her neck and shoulder muscles felt. She stretched her arms and the seat stretched with her.

There was silence for a moment while Laura made herself comfortable; then she realised that the detective, Sam, was looking at her curiously.

"What is it?" asked Laura.

"I'm sorry, was I staring? I was just trying to work out where you come from. You're certainly not a local girl are you?"

Laura was just about to reply that, 'yes, she was very much a local girl', when Doug arrived. He carried a tray with a jug and glass and a plate of what looked like mars bars.

"I thought you might be a bit hungry as well."

"Thanks, I am, but I'm afraid I don't have any food vouchers."

"Don't worry about that old sign," said Doug. "It's years out of date. We don't use those any more."

Laura realised she was very hungry indeed, not having eaten for ages. She was just wondering how she was going to balance the tray on her lap when Doug pressed his foot on the floor and a small circular section rose. When it reached the appropriate height for Laura's seat, he took his foot off and placed the tray beside her.

"There you are," he said. "Service with a smile."

"Wow, that was amazing!" said Laura. "I've never seen anything like that before."

Doug and Samantha looked at one another. He sat down in one of the other seats. The two detectives waited while Laura put her sketch book down and tucked in to the food and drink. She was so hungry that it disappeared in very quick time. Doug whistled. "Well, that's a healthy appetite you've got, haven't you?"

Laura smiled for the first time since she had found herself in the police building.

"Mmm," she said appreciatively. "That was very good, thank you. But I wasn't quite sure what kind of flavour that food had. Was it beef?"

"Beef!" repeated Doug. "Beef?" He shook his head.

"What's your name?" asked Samantha. "You don't mind me asking do you?"

"No of course not. It's Laura, Laura Trevillick."

"That's a nice name. Well, Laura, we haven't had any beef, or any sort of meat at all, for a long, long time. What you had in those bars was a kind of processed soya."

Laura sat still and thought hard – what had the policewoman meant; no beef in a long, long time?

"Do you mind if I ask you some questions Laura?"

"No, no not at all, help yourself."

20

"That's great. First one then. How old are you?"

"I'm 12."

"And what's your date of birth?"

"2nd of August, 1997."

Doug, who had been listening to this exchange stood up.

"Come again?" he asked.

Laura repeated the date "2nd of August, 1997." Then she said "Could I ask something?"

"The policewoman smiled. "Of course you may."

"Why aren't you writing anything down?"

"We haven't written anything down in years Laura. That can be open to all sorts of abuse. Everything we say and do is digitally recorded, visually and aurally, so that there is an accurate record of whatever takes place in the interview rooms. Any written transcription, if it is required, can be automatically done. At any rate there will be a permanent record on Computer's systems. Now, may I ask you some more questions? After all we want to find out why it is that you think you're lost."

Laura nodded, feeling somewhat bewildered.

"Good girl. Now, where do you live?"

"I live in a lovely village in Cornwall called St Wenver, right in the heart of Bodmin Moor."

Again there was a pause. Samantha and Doug exchanged 'those' looks; then Sam rose from her chair and pressed the palm of her hand against the wall. A screen lit up and the detective spoke to it.

"On visuals," she said. "Archive photo of Saint Wenver, Bodmin, circa 2009."

Almost immediately four pictures appeared on screen. Sam beckoned Laura over.

"Touch the picture which is most familiar to you," she said.

Laura reached forward and touched the third picture in the sequence. The screen filled out with an enlargement. Laura recognised the centre of the village.

"That's it!" she exclaimed. "That's where I live, or very near."

She turned triumphantly to the young woman beside her.

"You can get me home now, can't you?"

Samantha was eyeing her quizzically

"That might be just a little bit difficult. Archive, current photo of the same area."

The screen went blank and after a second or two was replaced by a scene which caused Laura to stagger back in dismay. It was just a vast mass of water. Nothing else. Just water.

Chapter 5

"There must be some mistake," said Laura, desperate for this to be the case.

An exclamation from Doug stopped Samantha from replying. She and Laura both turned to see Doug staring intently at the sketch book which he had open in his hands.

"Are these all your pictures Laura?" he asked.

"Yes, they're mine. I'm very fond of sketching."

Doug stared at Laura intently.

"Some of these pictures are a bit more than just sketches," he said. "I guess this must be a self portrait for example."

Laura and Samantha walked over and looked at the page Doug was holding for them.

"Wow, that is beautiful Laura," said Samantha. "And just like you."

The picture in question was, indeed, a portrait of Laura, but Laura had no idea how it got there. She seized the book.

"That isn't my drawing!" she said and began leafing back towards the beginning of the book. She gave a sigh of relief.

"These are all mine."

She showed Samantha and Doug the sheets at the front of the book. Flicking through the front half of the book they could both see that they reflected scenes of life in and around the Cornwall that she knew and loved.

"These are lovely too," said Samantha. "Where did you get the ideas for these pictures?"

"Oh, usually just from walking around the countryside. They're not all from St Wenver. We've travelled all over Cornwall."

Doug and Samantha exchanged 'looks' again; then Doug turned again to the portrait of Laura.

"So if this isn't a self-portrait, who did it?"

Laura stared at the picture. It was almost like staring at a photo of herself. The detail was perfect. Young as she was, Laura could really appreciate the talented hand that created the portrait.

"I've absolutely no idea who has drawn that," was all that she could think of to say.

"The picture is signed," pointed out Doug. "Look, there's the signature. Do you recognise it?"

Laura looked at the bottom of the page. She stared at the signature for a few seconds. Doug turned the book back to the front cover. Underneath the title "My Sketch Book" was Laura's signature. It was identical to the one beneath the portrait.

Shaken, Laura looked at the detectives.

"I...I don't understand."

"There's something else here, that I don't understand either," went on Doug relentlessly. He turned back to the portrait of Laura and then turned the page again. Here there was an equally good portrait – but this time of Detective Samantha Flick. Now it was Samantha's turn to gasp.

"Jeepers Creepers!" she exclaimed. "How in Computer did that get there?"

Laura shook her head. "I don't know," was all she could think of. How could she say it happened while she was asleep in a strange house? An establishment that did not appear to exist in this place?

Samantha took Laura by the hand and sat her down again.

"Laura," she began. "You said you were born in 1990…?"

"1997. On 2nd August, 1997."

Doug's facial muscles tightened.

"So, what year do you think it is now?" he asked.

"Well, 2009 of course. What else would it be?"

The two detectives got up and walked to the other side of the room where they became immersed in conversation. Laura looked around the room as they talked. She could see no sign of the door through which she had entered. She was as effectively locked in as she had been in that house. She thought that she might have heard the words 'unbalanced' and 'doctor' from the whispering going on between Doug and Samantha. Then, without speaking to her, Doug left the room via a gap that appeared in the wall as he approached it. Laura wondered if she would be able to leave just as easily or did each police officer have some special piece of equipment that enabled the bearer to move about without restraint. Samantha, meanwhile, remained standing pensively.

"Well," asked Laura. "If it's not 2009, what year is it?"

Samantha came and sat down close to Laura. She took her hand.

"Are you sure you want to know?"

Laura nodded. There was a big sigh from the detective. She stood up and walked over to the screen

"Reveal today's date," she snapped.

The screen blanked then flashed some figures. Laura's eyes widened.

"It can't be," she said. "That's impossible."

The date on the screen read 'August 1st 3009'.

Chapter 6

"It's a mistake," said Laura. "Your computer's up the spout. I don't believe it. That's nonsense."

She had got up and was shouting at the screen. When there was no response she banged her hands at the screen in some kind of futile attempt to make the date change back. All that happened was that the screen disappeared and Laura's hands were slapping at the wall.

The door slid open again and Doug re-entered, this time accompanied by an older man. Like Doug he was uniformed, but to Laura's artistic eye there was something different about him. He seemed less militaristic.

Gently, Samantha led Laura back to her chair where, with equal gentleness she was persuaded to sit down.

"This is Dr Sternman. He's here to help sort this out."

Laura looked at the doctor. He was quite tall, but with a slight stoop to his shoulders. His eyes were a deep brown. They appeared to be the only gentle things in his otherwise severe, lined face.

Doug showed him the sketchbook. Dr Sternman looked through it carefully. He paused over the sketches at the front.

"These are yours?" he asked and when Laura nodded, he added "Yes, very pleasant. You have a real talent and an excellent imagination."

He continued studying the book, oblivious to Laura's blushes. He looked closely at the portraits and pored over them very carefully, occasionally peering at the young girl. After a while he closed the book.

"Tell me Laura, do you know how these other drawings got in to your sketch book?"

Laura shook her head, tears springing to her eyes – though whether from anger or self pity or just fear, she could not be sure.

The doctor smiled patiently and as he did so his entire facial appearance changed. For a moment the stern features became kind, almost radiant. Then the smile disappeared and he became serious again.

"Clearly, we have some dilemma here. It is quite obvious, even to an untrained eye, that you have talent. But do you have the talent to produce portraits such as these? Oh yes, the signature appears to be yours, but it is possible for such things to be forged. However, certain aspects of your early sketches can also be detected in the very fine detail shown in these pictures." He turned once again to the portrait of Laura, and then turned over to the portraits of Samantha and Doug. "The mystery is compounded by the excellent representations of my two colleagues here, and again, in spite of the signatures, I am convinced that you could not possibly have drawn these by accident. My feeling, therefore, is that somebody else is responsible for these and we will have to borrow your book, young lady, for some further tests and analysis."

He saw the look of alarm on Laura's face.

"But, let me assure you, before we see any more tears or tantrums, that the utmost care will be taken of your property and it will be returned to you unblemished. We will even see that you have a proper receipt for it. I will leave that up to you Detective Flick."

Without waiting for a reply or confirmation from Samantha, he got up from his seat and stood over Laura.

"I'm going to ask you now to accompany me to my office so that I can examine you properly and ask some more questions. Is that clear?"

Laura looked at Samantha, alarm written all over her face. The detective smiled.

"Don't worry. It's routine in cases like this. And I'll come with you in any case, so there's nothing to be frightened of."

She gripped Laura's arm and helped her to her feet.

"Ready?"

Laura nodded even though she did not feel in the least bit ready. Nevertheless, she allowed herself to be escorted across the room. A panel slid aside. Laura hesitated. The space revealed was very small.

"Come along, come along," said the doctor impatiently." It's only an elevator. Doug, take the sketchbook to F1 for analysis and don't forget to get a receipt!"

They were inside the elevator with the panel closing before Laura had time to think about protesting After all, it was still her property.

There was a slight shuddering movement, barely noticeable, but Laura had no way of knowing whether they were moving up, down or sideways.

Chapter 7

Dr Sternman noticed Laura's discomfort.

"Don't worry," he said. "We're going down. All the offices and dwellings are well below ground level."

Laura was puzzled.

"What about all those tall buildings I passed on my way here?"

Samantha answered her query.

"Those aren't offices at all. They're the source from which we get our power supplies. Each one of those tall buildings is a solar collecting point. You could say that they're like giant batteries."

Laura wasn't sure she wanted to ask her next question.

"Is that the only power supply you have?"

Samantha smiled. "Relax; the lift is not going to get stuck. We never run out of power. The sun is a very reliable source."

Laura had so many questions now throbbing through her brain that before she could select the right one, the elevator came to a halt.

"My office is just along here. Come along young lady."

The doctor led the way briskly. There was no way of knowing where the door to Dr Sternman's office was as the walls appeared uniformly flat. There were no handles to be seen anywhere. They stopped at a part of the wall which had no apparent markings. Dr Sternman placed his hand flat against the wall.

-'Welcome back to your office doctor,' – The computer voice that spoke was similar to the one that Laura had heard in the square. A panel slid aside and they walked into a surprisingly large room which housed a desk, some of the hanging chairs that Laura had encountered in Samantha's area and an elaborately curved couch.

Dr Sternman sat behind his desk while Laura and Samantha sat in the other two available seats on the opposite side. The doctor pressed part of the surface of his desk.

"This is Dr Sternman interviewing our visitor to Bodmin City State, Miss Laura Trevillick." His brown eyes peered at his subject. "Laura, I want you to tell me all about yourself, in your own words and in your own time." He smiled rather humourlessly. "Forgive the choice of words, they weren't meant to be funny. Now, while you're speaking I want you to hold this in either one of your hands. Grip it firmly. That's it."

There was a pause as Laura tried to reflect on what she had learned so far, but once again, before she had any real chance to formulate her thoughts the doctor was prompting her: "Well, go on then, off you go. Just speak normally. Your words will be automatically recorded."

Laura began speaking rather quietly at which point the doctor firmly instructed her to speak up.

"My name is Laura Trevillick," she began again. "I was born on 2nd August, 1997 at Treliske Maternity unit near Truro, near where we lived in Cusgarne. We've recently moved to St Wenver, to a house with a separate studio. My parents are Robert and Sarah

Trevillick. My father is in the navy and is away at sea...." Laura faltered here. If the date she had seen was true, then her father would no longer be at sea. In fact, he wouldn't be anywhere. Laura raised her hands to her face.

"Please continue Laura." said Dr Sternman. "I realise that this must be difficult for you, but in order to help you we must go through this very necessary process. Do you understand?"

Laura nodded and continued.

"My mother is a sculptress. She's very good. She's the one that uses the studio for her work. I attend Liskeard School. I have no brothers or sisters. But we do have two cats, Freddie and Rosie, Popeye – he's a parrot, and Snowy, my rabbit."

Dr Sternman held up his hand. He studied a screen on his desk. Then he sat back in his seat, folding his arms as he did so.

"That's very interesting," he said.

"I thought it was very ordinary," said Laura. "Almost boring even."

The doctor smiled.

"No, it's not your account itself that is interesting me; it's what Computer is telling me that I find so fascinating."

Now it was Samantha's turn to look puzzled.

"Well, what is the computer telling you Doctor?"

Instead of answering, he pursed his lips and swung his chair so that he was now facing the wall of his office.

"Look at this Laura," he said.

From his pocket he took a small gadget; it looked to Laura like some form of remote control. He pressed on the box and immediately a scene was displayed right across the wall, facing all three people in the room. It showed a beach with waves crashing onto rocks and spumes of spray splashing towards them. Laura stood up.

"Oh that's lovely. It's like the sea at Gwithian."

"It looks real doesn't it?" said Dr Sternman.

"Yes, oh yes… you can almost smell the fresh air."

"Unfortunately, like much of what goes on here, it's only a pictorial scene. Here's another one I like."

He touched the box again and this time there were horses thundering across a plain. Turning back to look at Laura he asked:

"Do you have horses near where you live?"

"Not like those horses," laughed Laura. "But, yes, there are quite a few horses in or near our village. My mother used to ride a lot."

The doctor was studying the screen on his desk again. The scene behind him vanished; replaced by the blank, shiny walls.

"That's true as well," he said.

"What?" Laura was puzzled.

"Everything you have told me has been verified by the detector as being one hundred per cent true."

Laura was shocked.

"Did you think I was lying?"

Samantha touched her arm gently.

"You have to remember Laura, the shock you had when I showed you today's date. Well, now it's our turn to be shocked."

Laura slumped in her chair.

"But I don't understand."

The doctor rose from his chair, walked to Laura and removed the device that she was still gripping tightly. He smiled a confused, slightly sad smile.

"The truth is, Laura, we don't understand either."

Gently he pulled her to her feet and walked her over to his couch.

"Would you mind getting on to this couch please; there are one or two very minor tests I'd like to have carried out, none of which will hurt or be in any way invasive. Are you happy with that?"

He seemed so kind that, in spite of her misgiving, Laura lay on the couch. She felt it adjust to her body. It was a most comfortable feeling. Dr Sternman pressed a switch at the side and a small drawer opened. He removed what looked like a glove which had a tube running into part of the interior of the couch. Carefully he placed Laura's hand inside the glove. The same sense of adjustment took place.

"This glove is a very useful piece of equipment. It can conduct a number of tests, from which we can determine your DNA, blood pressure, blood count and along with other statistics and more importantly, the general state of your health. And, what's more, it does all this in seconds. In fact, here are the results already to hand."

Laura had only felt a slight tingling. The doctor removed the glove and returned it to its compartment, and then sat back at his desk contemplating the information being relayed. Meanwhile, Samantha helped Laura down. When they were both seated again the doctor spoke to the computer.

"Audio on," he said. He then spoke directly to Laura.

"What you will hear may disturb you or even frighten you. Just remember that Detective Flick and I are on hand to help you and, hopefully, to reassure you. Computer, relay the information concerning Laura Trevillick."

Immediately the voice that Laura had now come to accept as part of this strange system began its monologue.

"Subject's blood was tested. She is a healthy female, age 12. Blood pressure and blood count are both well within normal levels. Heart rate was a little high at the time of testing but returned to normal very quickly. DNA results confirm that she is Laura Trevillick, who, according to computer records was born on August 2nd, 1997. As the current year is 3009 there is clearly an anomaly here. What is even more surprising, but of great scientific significance, is the presence at the Research Institute, of an adult female in her seventies, also currently undergoing observation, who, according to similar tests carried out, is also Laura Trevillick. Paintings and portraits by the adult Trevillick were highly collectable in the early part of the twenty first century. Furthermore, tests recently completed on the sketchbook belonging to the younger subject confirm the signatures and drawings as being genuine. The portraits found in the sketchbook are also perfect specimens of the techniques used by the artist in question, though, interestingly, they have never been catalogued, suggesting that they have only recently been completed. The existence of two people both identified as Laura Trevillick is outside our normal range of expectation and further investigation is required. It is recommended that procedures be carried out with caution."

Chapter 8

Laura, who had grown even paler than her normal fair complexion, was utterly confused and amazed simultaneously. How could she be here in 3009 at the same time as a much older self was also being investigated? But if the experience was happening to her, and therefore possible, then surely it was possible for an older 'self' to also be stranded in this time?

"You can appreciate," the doctor's words interrupted her thoughts. "How interested we are to discover not one, but two Laura Trevillicks in our midst. As yet we have no satisfactory explanations. The older Trevillick is being accommodated in the research institute. Like you she has undergone tests and is still under observation."

Laura did not know what to make of these revelations and she wondered if the terms 'accommodated' and 'under observation' were polite words for 'imprisonment'.

"Would I be able to meet this other Laura?"

The doctor closed his eyes and rubbed his temples. This was a situation he had never encountered. It was incredible, and what was its significance? Would it have repercussions in this world of 3009 which could disturb the delicate balance of life on this threatened planet or would it prove, ultimately, to be beneficial to the vastly different society of the 31st century?

He opened his eyes and stared at Laura. She seemed so innocent as well as ignorant of the turbulent one thousand years of history that separated her two existences.

"From an experimental point of view, as a scientist, I would certainly appreciate being present at such a meeting. As a doctor, however, I must agree with Computer and proceed with caution."

"Why's that?" asked Laura apprehensively, fearing that there might be something wrong with her older self.

"Well, one of you is problematical enough, but two of you, of different ages and appearance certainly, but, nevertheless, clearly manifestations of the same person, could cause a spatial anomaly in this our time. Who knows what consequences such an event might precipitate?"

"But Dr Sternman," interrupted Samantha. "If one of the Lauras has already appeared, and now this one – maybe there's some purpose to it all. Maybe they are meant to meet."

The detective smiled sympathetically at Laura.

"I'm sorry," she said. "We're talking about you as if you're not here with us. But you've got to understand – we have responsibilities towards the citizens of Bodmin City State. The situation needs to be handled delicately."

""We also have a responsibility towards you, young lady," went on the doctor. "After all we would want to find out if it is at all possible for you to return to your own time."

The thought of being stuck in the year 3009, in a concrete city, for the rest of her life, was horrifying. Laura stood up.

"If there's a chance that meeting this …. other me, might allow us both to return to our own times, wouldn't that be something worth trying? Please."

Doctor Sternman frowned, but, after some moments his face relaxed.

"You have some wonderful qualities Laura Trevillick, and so, while we will do our best to find out how we might be instrumental in fulfilling your wish, I must also add that if, as seems possible, you are here for some time, at least you would be a marvellous asset to our city."

"What - like some sort of guinea pig you mean?"

The doctor shook his head.

"No, of course not. What you have yet to learn is that our youth, our children have lost that vitality and energy of which you have an abundant supply." He stood up. "Come then, let's visit the other Laura. Let's throw caution to the wind. Let us grasp the nettle!"

He strode forward decisively, collecting Laura and Samantha on his way and pressed another part of the wall. They passed through into another corridor, identical to the one they had used before. Laura was confused but decided to keep her thoughts to herself.

As they were proceeding, a panel slid open and a tall, sallow-skinned man dressed almost entirely in black, stepped through, blocking their way.

"Sternman, Detective Flick," he acknowledged, but his gaze was fixed on Laura. "And this must be our newest arrival, Laura Trevillick – the younger."

Dr Sternman nodded, almost imperceptibly.

"Laura, this is Mr Millar. He is head of our security and surveillance team. No doubt he has been monitoring your presence in BCS since your arrival here earlier."

"Naturally. It would be a dereliction of my duty were I to ignore such unique circumstances."

Dr Sternman and Millar stood glaring at one another in mutual animosity. Samantha interrupted their eyeball to eyeball confrontation.

"Shall we continue gentlemen? I expect Laura's rather anxious to meet our, er, other guest."

"Of course." Mr Millar's smile was not the least bit pleasant. "Lead on please detective, with all haste."

Sensing the awkwardness now present since Mr Millar's arrival, Laura followed on directly behind Samantha, the only person there with whom she felt safe.

They came to a halt and an elevator door opened.

"How do you know where all the entrances and exits are?" Laura whispered.

Samantha shrugged. "I guess it's just something we all get used to. We learn to navigate our way round from an early age."

Once again Laura was unsure of the direction they were travelling in, nor could she work out how the elevator knew which way they wished to go. Part of her wanted to find out as much as she could about this strange city state; but a larger part simply yearned to return home. She tried to avoid thinking about meeting a much older version of herself. The elevator door opened.

"Here we are," said Dr Sternman. "The Research Institute, where we shall see what we shall see."

"Have we just travelled underground?" Laura asked Samantha.

"Yes, it's much quicker and much safer. We were very surprised when you came in the entrance that you did. Hardly anyone goes outside these days. The sun's UV rays can be very dangerous."

Laura touched her skin, alarmed that she might unwittingly have placed herself in danger. Seeing this, Samantha continued: "It's fine. The scans you had on entering both the city entrance and our headquarters would have neutralised any damage. Had you been out there too long the alarm system would have notified us of any problems."

Before Laura could ask any further questions they had arrived at a large screen.

"Welcome," said the familiar computer voice. "To the Institute for Research and development. Please press your hands to the screen for identification purposes."

As each person did so they were individually welcomed by name. When Laura put her hand in place she wondered what would happen and was relieved by the perfectly ordinary response of "Welcome, Laura Trevillick."

"Don't look so surprised, "said Dr Sternman. "Computer has already assimilated all your details from the examination in my office. You can now go anywhere you like in the city and Computer's systems will be there to guide you."

"Almost anywhere…" added Mr Millar.

Computer's voice interrupted any further discussion. "Dr Chang will meet you on level five. I hope you have a pleasant visit."

Another elevator ride took them to level 5 where a young, anxious looking man was waiting. He was much shorter than either of the other two males.

"Ah, welcome to you all. How nice to see you again Dr Sternman, Detective Flick.....Mr Millar." He must have been prepared to meet Laura, but still his eyes registered surprise when he saw her. He walked around her and then peered closely at her features. She felt his warm breath on her face – it was not unpleasant though.

"Remarkable," said Dr Chang. "Most remarkable. Please, follow me now and we will endeavour to discover if it is possible for this young lady to meet ... that other lady."

Laura was disappointed to discover that the décor here was no different to the areas she had so recently visited. The walls were the same plain silvery colour. She touched a wall. It was warm to her touch. As her fingers pressed against it a small panel slid open and Computer's voice spoke.

"Laura Trevillick. Your nutrition levels are low. Please eat the enclosed food bar."

Laura looked round in surprise. Samantha giggled.

"You'll have to eat it now; otherwise Computer will pester you until you do." Seeing Laura hesitate she added "Go on, it's quite safe and will provide you with all the essentials your body needs."

Laura took the 'food bar' from the space within the wall. The panel slid shut. She took a small bite and chewed it well. The flavour was fairly bland, but not unpleasant.

"Come along, eat as you go," said Dr Chang, chivvying everyone along.

By the time they reached yet another screen, Laura had eaten her way through the snack. She certainly felt more energised and more alert. A screen 'Welcome' was followed by "Our visitor is comfortable and may be viewed." The scene now revealed on-screen showed someone standing by an easel, painting.

"Well Laura," said Dr Sternman. "What's it like to see yourself as a more mature person?"

The woman clearly showed a strong resemblance to the young girl peering intently at the image. The shape of the face – colour of her eyes. – 'And still painting, how wonderful,' – thought Laura.

"Does she know I'm here?" she asked.

Dr Chang shook his head.

"I have waited to meet you first, to reassure myself that you are ready. You seem very level headed. Before you go in I will speak with her. If you wait across here for the moment."

A panel slid open to reveal a waiting room where the wall panels displayed fish swimming in a coral sea. Dr Chang walked to the opposite wall and was about to place his palm against it when Computer spoke again

"Warning! Warning! Subject's vital signs are fluctuating. Proceed with caution."

On hearing these words everyone in the waiting room got up from their seats and ran towards Dr Chang who was attempting to gain entry.

"Computer, the panel is not opening. Explain!"

"Warning! Warning! Subject's vital signs are.....Subject's vital signs have disappeared."

The panel now slid open. The room was empty. As they all rushed in Laura felt her heart beating anxiously for her other self.

"Damnation!" said Mr Millar. "She's vanished. Completely. Gone into thin air!"

The rest of the party stood round the spot where Laura's other self had been standing, painting, their backs towards Laura. Something caused her to look over her shoulder. An oak door appeared in the wall. Without thinking Laura raced towards it and as she did so it clicked open for her. She ran through into the upstairs hall which she had seen before with its familiar wall coverings and its large mirror.

-'Welcome back, Laura.'-

Without replying she ran down the stairs and across to the main door.

"Please open for me, please open."

It obliged her and soon she was running down the familiar garden path. As she drew nearer to the gate she was astonished to see the children, whom she's almost forgotten about, still gathered there. They were jeering.

"Couldn't take it then, could you?" sneered John.

Laura's mouth dropped.

"Did you get frightened?" asked May. "I don't blame you for running back so soon. None of us have ever even gone through the gate, let alone gone up to the house."

Laura's mind was in a whirl. How could she be back here, exactly where she was, when she had just spent hours in Bodmin City State?

"I must get back home, I'm sorry."

She ran, then stopped, turned round and called "What year is it?"

There were more jeers, but May replied "It's 2009 of course – are you sure you're all right?"

Laura waved and then turned and flew down through the village as if pursued by hordes of wild things, not stopping until she had got to the converted barn they now called home. She continued running straight round to the studio in the back garden and burst through the door. Her mother was there with clay on her hands as she struggled with her latest creation.

"Laura?" she looked up in surprise. Before she could say another word, her daughter was there in her arms, holding her tight.

Chapter 9

Later, over mugs of hot chocolate and rich tea biscuits, perfect for dunking, Laura and her mother were chatting about the day's events.

"I had a phone call from your father; he sends you his love and hopes you're behaving yourself."

Mrs Trevillick giggled; a youthful sound. She'd laughed to herself really, because Laura had been one of the best-behaved girls she had ever come across. Parties, either here, or at the homes of friends, usually gave children opportunities to behave in the worst possible manner. She could quite easily imagine any number of boys of her acquaintance who could easily sink to the anarchic levels of the Lord of the Fly gangs, given half the chance. Laura, however, had never sulked or indulged in tantrums, was always pleased with any present she received and, even better, a sound sleeper at night. She was looking forward to her daughter's continuing growth, both academically – she was doing well at school – and artistically; already she was showing signs of much promise.

"What are you grinning at mum?" asked Laura.

"I'm just thinking how lucky I am to have such a lovely daughter. Big day tomorrow too; 13 years old!" She scrabbled her daughter's hair. "Now, come on, enough of all this sentimentality; go and fetch your sketchbook. I'd like to see what you've been doing today."

The sight of her daughter, gaping at her like a fish out of water, caused mild alarm.

"What is it? You haven't lost it, have you?"

"I'm...." Laura paused, unsure of what to say. She had always been open and honest with both her parents, but to tell the truth now seemed difficult, if not impossible. Her mother would laugh at her, or worse, think that she had lost her mind.

"I'm...not sure. I...I left it somewhere. Oh, it's alright," she added, seeing her mother's concern. "I know where it is; I'm just not sure if I'll be able to get it back."

"What on earth are you talking about? That doesn't make any sense at all. Have you left it at a friend's house? Have you made some friends here?"

Laura, who was as anxious as her mother to retrieve the sketch book, got up quickly.

"In fact, I do know exactly where it is. I'll see if I can get it now."

She rushed up to her mum, gave her a hug and quick kiss on the cheek and then was running and running back towards the old house.

"Laura," called her mother. "Don't be back late."

Her daughter waved, but kept running. Mrs Trevillick frowned and pensively returned to her studio in order to continue her own art work.

Laura reached the house. The other children had disappeared, so that was a relief. She had to retrieve her sketchbook, but would the house allow her back in; and even if it did, would she be able to get back into the same time, the same moment that she had so recently left? She checked her watch – it was still only three o'clock in the afternoon. Taking a deep breath, Laura ran down the garden path towards the front door.

Chapter 10

Laura was standing by the massive oak structure that was the entrance to a whole new world. Would it respond to her again or was entry only allowed once in a lifetime? She turned and looked back at the garden, breathing in the warmth of summer, fixing in her mind all visible signs of her reality. As before, the gate seemed a long way down the path, further, surely, than she had actually run. A bird flew down and sat on the gate, fluffing its wings. "Please be there when I get back," thought Laura.

Then, having made up her mind she forced herself to face the door again. It was open. "Thank you," she said and walked in; everything appeared unchanged. She ran across the hall, up the stairs, across the upper gallery, past the mirror where her image waved at her, though Laura herself had not done so, and then at last arrived at the other door. She ran at it, expecting almost, to hurt her face in the rush, but she was through and to her utter delight in the same place, the same room with Samantha, Dr Sternman, Dr Chang and Mr Millar still standing round the painting. The impetus of running through the door propelled her forward and she ran straight into Mr Millar. He looked at her, startled. Then his sharp eyes took in her flushed appearance and heavy breathing. The others also turned to stare at Laura, but it was Mr Millar who spoke first.

"What made you run across the room like that?" he asked suspiciously.

He did not wait for a reply but walked back to the wall which Laura was relieved to see was its normal silvery self, with no trace of solid wood door, locked or otherwise. Mr Millar touched the wall. A panel slid open and he peered out into the corridor. He faced Laura again and stared hard at her.

"Did you just run out of this room and then back in again? Have you been playing games with us?"

"Don't be ridiculous, Millar," said Dr Sternman, almost contemptuously. "Why on earth would she have done that? Come here Laura, look at this and tell me if it is familiar to you."

Laura came and stood beside him. She recognised the scene at once. It was the garden through which she had just passed. Another world, another place.

"It's very near to where I live," she said. "I recognised it at once. It's a beautiful painting."

"You should be proud of yourself," Millar remarked sarcastically. "It is, after all, your own work. Eventually."

Samantha tactfully changed the subject.

"Dr Chang, is there any way of finding out how the subject disappeared so suddenly?"

Dr Chang struggled not to look confused.

"There is a mystery here involving Laura Trevillick. It was difficult enough to find an explanation when we had only one such person. Then when a second, but younger version appeared that doubled our problems. Now, one of the two has vanished and so the variables multiply. Ai, who knows what will happen next! I have never come across such phenomena before. How can I attempt any explanations or conduct experiments when we are dealing with the unknown?"

He flapped his arms helplessly.

"What does the computer say about it?" asked Laura.

All eyes in the room focused on her.

"Well, well," said Mr Millar. "Isn't there an old saying 'Out of the mouths of babies....'?"

"It's 'babes' actually," said Laura. "And I'm not a baby anyway."

"Never mind the old sayings, it's still a good idea, and I'm sure someone would eventually have thought of it. Computer," demanded Dr Sternman. "Where did Laura Trevillick go?"

'Thank you for the question, Dr Sternman, but to which Laura were you referring?'

"The one that has disappeared of course."

'I am unable to determine where that Laura has gone. She is not present in this time any longer.'

Dr Sternman grunted.

"What about you Chang, do you want to try your luck with Computer?"

"Yes, thank you Dr Sternman. Computer. Did the older Laura disappear as a result of the younger girl's imminent approach?"

'The probability of that occurrence would appear to be high Dr Chang.'

Mr Millar grabbed hold of Laura's arm.

"In that case," he said emphatically. "I think it's time security took charge of this since you scientists, so called, do not seem to have a clue what you are doing."

"And what good do you suppose that would do," said Dr Sternman. "Are you just going to keep her locked up for the duration?"

"What an excellent idea doctor; that would do nicely I should think, for the time being."

Laura attempted to pull her arm free.

"Excuse me," she said. "You're all treating me as if I don't exist."

"Precisely! You don't exist here in this time. And because you don't exist here you constitute a threat to our entire city state."

"Why? What possible harm could I do?" She finally succeeded in wrenching her arm from Millar's grasp. "Dr Sternman?"

Dr Sternman rubbed the back of his neck. He was clearly struggling to find the right way forward.

"Laura, Laura…your appearance, and that of your older self also, may not in themselves appear threatening, but it is possible that having materialised here the danger to our society and our way of life if you should return to your own time, may prove quite alarming."

"But how, doctor? I like you all…" Mr Millar snorted. "Well, almost all, why would I do anything to harm you?"

"Look let's go back to my office and sit down together and I will attempt to explain the situation. Is that a reasonable proposition Mr Millar?"

"As long as you take full responsibility if anything goes wrong, Doctor."

Doctor Sternman took Laura's arm, though in a more gentle fashion.

"Fine; I accept full responsibility. If you will all accompany me to my office then perhaps we can come to some appropriate arrangement."

Chapter 11

When they all arrived in Dr Sternman's office, Laura was surprised to see that there were enough chairs for everyone. She was sure that there had only been three of the hanging chairs during her last visit. She wondered if 'Computer' was able to adapt rooms to suit whoever was going to be present.

"Before I begin," said Dr Sternman. "Would anyone like any refreshment?"

Nobody took up the offer.

"Come on Sternman," said Mr Millar. "Let's not waste any more valuable time; get on with your explanation so that I can get on with my investigation."

There was a distinct note of menace in Millar's last few words and Laura felt increasingly uncomfortable in his presence. She tried, therefore, to ignore the security officer and, instead, to concentrate on whatever Dr Sternman had to say.

"Well," he said. "We have a most unusual, if not unique situation, here in our city, perhaps even in our entire inhabited planet. Our previous 'guest' had appeared in the same mysterious way that young Laura herself came to our attention. Unlike you, Laura, she just appeared one day with her paints and easel in one of the vacant rooms of the Institute for Research and, in spite of all our enquiries we were unable to determine how she had arrived. Dr Chang had been observing her and noted how at ease she was, how comfortable she was with her surroundings and how co-operative she was in most ways."

"Co-operative! What eyewash!" interrupted Mr Millar. "She refused to say how she got here; she answered any of my questions with questions of her own, pretended her ignorance of all technical matters and insisted on being allowed to get on with her own work. For all we know she could be a foreign agent seeking to usurp our city state. If I'd had my way...."

"Yes, yes, Mr Millar," said Dr Sternman, wearily. "We are all aware of your own rather dubious methods, which, I must remind you, most citizens of this state find distinctly old-fashioned."

"Sometimes the old-fashioned methods can produce significant results – look at the case of the cavers on level 153. Without my investigations our city state would have been seriously compromised; in fact, if they'd been allowed to continue their efforts thousands could have died in the resulting floods."

Laura did not have any idea about what Mr Millar was referring to, nor could she get her head around 'cavers on level 153'. Was that 153 levels below ground? Samantha interrupted her thoughts.

"That happened years ago. Surely you're not suggesting that Laura poses any thing like as serious a threat as those people?"

"That's the whole point!" Mr Millar was practically shouting. "We are waiting for our learned scientists to tell us just exactly what threat they think she is to our whole society. Well, Dr Sternman? Dr Chang?"

The two scientists exchanged eye contact. Dr Chang nodded.

"Very well," said Dr Sternman. "Let me try to explain as simply as possible so that everyone understands. Laura here and earlier on, her older self, appeared out of thin air apparently, both of them unaware of how they got here."

He now addressed Laura directly.

"The danger to our society is that you have come from a time one thousand years in our past, from a time of plenty; from a time when people lived on the earth, rather than beneath it; from a time when there was an abundance of food; from a time when humankind was in control, more or less. Now let us suppose that you are able to return to that time, as seems likely given the disappearance of your older self. What might happen as a result of your visit?"

"Why should anything happen?" asked Laura.

"That's why we need to consider the matter. Let's say that you are able to return to your own time and that other scientists discover what you have done and what you have found here in the 31st century. They might come to the conclusion that things must be done to change the future. And what would be the repercussions on us if they succeeded?"

"But that would be impossible," said Laura. "How can I change anything? I'm just 12 years old. Who's going to believe a word I say?"

The doctor smiled patiently.

"They might not believe you, but they would certainly take more notice of a considerably older person."

"Even so, how can anything change something that is already here?"

Before anyone else could say any more there was a loud chime and a screen lit up on the wall.

'It is approaching 2200 hours. Quarters have been prepared for Miss Laura Trevillick. It is suggested that Detective Flick accompany her to these quarters. Lights will be dimmed at 2200 hours to preserve power. Have a good rest everybody.'

"Thank you Computer," hissed Mr Millar. "Spot on as usual." He stood up and leaned down towards Laura.

"Get a good night's rest Miss Trevillick. Tomorrow you and I will have a private chat when I will have my say."

Laura tried to avoid his eyes. If she was going to have a private chat, Mr Millar would be the last person with whom she would wish to engage. The very thought of such a meeting made her flesh creep.

Chapter 12

Samantha showed Laura to her quarters. Once again she was unsure of how her guide could lead the way in what appeared to be an unchangeable environment. They went through three elevator rides and several corridors before finally entering a room. Samantha showed Laura how to get her resting couch by pressing on a certain area on the wall. A bed slid out from a compartment.

"There we are," said Samantha. "Get yourself a good rest."

"What about Mr Millar?"

"Don't worry about him. He's got to sleep just like the rest of us. If you want anything just ask Computer. Sleep well."

Before Laura could ask any further questions the detective had slid through the door and was gone. The young girl ran to the wall and spread her hands over it, seeking some way to open that door again. Nothing happened. She ran across to another wall and tried again. Still nothing. Laura walked over to the bed and sat down. It felt very comfortable. Another panel slid open and a large bundle of material appeared.

"What do I do with this, make my own bed?" she exclaimed.

Laura thought she had been talking to herself but a well-known voice answered.

'This is your body wrap Laura Trevillick. If you remove all your own clothing and put this wrap on while you rest it will conform to your size and shape; it will move with you; it will absorb any unnecessary moisture and it will maintain the correct body temperature.'

"Is that you Computer?"

'Yes, Laura Trevillick, it is I, Computer. Is there anything further that you require?"

"Yes," said Laura, a little embarrassed. "Where's the toilet please?"

A panel slid open. Laura walked across and peered inside. There was a hole in what could be assumed to be a toilet seat, although it was still made of the same silvery metallic material from which the walls and floors were constructed. There was no toilet paper, no towel, and no wash basin. Laura was perplexed.

"Computer?"

'Yes, Laura Trevillick.'

"How do I use this?"

There was a pause. Then, having considered the question, Computer resumed:

'Remove all your clothing and place it on the floor. Your clothes will be cleaned and prepared for after rest. Enter this area and sit on the seat. When you have completed the process the room will seal, the seat will retract and you will be washed, cleaned and dried. Is that clear Laura Trevillick?'

Laura felt as if she was being treated like a child, but, in need of the 'facilities' she hastily obeyed. Soon her clothes were in a bundle by her feet and, rather tremulously, she entered the room and sat down. Having completed the necessary steps as quickly as possible she stood and waited for the next stage. Before she had a chance to feel uncomfortable, jets of foamy liquid washed over her for several seconds. Laura was about to squeal when the jets ceased and warm air flowed around her, quickly drying her all over. The experience was, unusual, but not unpleasant.

When the door opened again Laura stepped out feeling fluffy and refreshed. She walked over to her bed and slipped the body wrap on. It seemed to adjust itself to her body and she suddenly felt very comfortable and also very sleepy. She lay down on the bed.

'Sleep well, Laura Trevillick.'

"Thank you Computer," said Laura, and fell asleep.

While Laura slept, the walls of her room changed to reveal a night sky, a dark, blue-black sky. Slowly, almost one by one, pinpoints of light appeared. Gradually, stars spread around the room, glimmering and winking – a universe of secret light. As Computer became aware that Laura's consciousness was beginning to move out of sleep mode, the stars grew dimmer as dawn ebbed slowly from the base of the room, creeping up into a brilliant burst of sunlight. Just as Laura showed signs of awakening, the glorious display faded and vanished; a private display for a sleeping child, a wonder that melted into silver walls just as Laura awoke, fully refreshed with no idea of what she had just missed. Was this a cruel joke played on an unsuspecting human, or a secret symphony conducted by a wistful soul?

Laura breakfasted on a food bar and a tub of liquid – 'Full of all the essential vitamins, nutrients and minerals that a growing girl requires' – confirmed Computer. Once again she used the interesting toilet facilities, was washed, showered and dried and couldn't help wondering if that was the procedure every time any one wanted to 'spend a penny'?

She found that her clothes had been cleaned and aired, but whether this was through some human agency or as a result of Computer's wizardry, she had no idea. When she was dressed a panel slid open. To her dismay, Laura saw that Mr Millar was waiting for her. Had he been there all night? Had he slept on her doorstep, so to speak? She felt her lips twitch at the thought – but Mr Millar's clothing appeared as clean and crumple-free as her own.

"I trust you slept well Miss Trevillick?" he said, but even this innocuous remark had a sinister ring to it. Laura waited to see if he would come, uninvited, into her room, but he remained outside, hovering, as though unwilling, or, indeed, unable to enter. Laura turned her back on him.

"Computer," she whispered. "Can anyone else enter this room?"

'Only if they are invited in.'

"So, Mr Millar, can't just, sort of, barge in on me?"

'Oh no! That would be most impolite. Besides, if he did attempt such an action, he would be subject to severe punishment.'

Thus reassured, Laura turned round, beamed at Mr Millar and said "Good Morning, and thank you, yes, I slept really well."

Chapter 13

Some moments later, Laura dutifully followed Mr Millar into his office, a room no different in any way to the few she had already seen. After she had sat down though, he pressed a button on his desk and the silver walls changed to display a busy city centre scene, with crowds of people hurrying in different directions. As she looked around the 360 degree panorama, Laura realised that the impression was of being in the midst of a typical day around Piccadilly Circus in London, for there, surely, was the famous statue of Eros. Mr Millar, meanwhile, was studying different parts of the view and staring intently as if trying to pick out someone in particular or even to engage the shoppers in conversation.

"Magnificent, isn't it?" he said at last. "All these people congregating in one place, hurrying from shop to shop or travelling on auto vehicles – all above ground. Marvellous!"

Laura looked again carefully and decided that what he referred to as 'auto vehicles' were, in fact, London buses.

"Have you ever been to this city, Miss Trevillick?"

"London?" she asked.

He nodded, almost eagerly.

"Only once, with my parents; we went about two years ago." She stopped suddenly, seeing Mr Millar's raised eyebrows.

"Oh, sorry, I mean in my own time, of course, in 2007. My parents were very good, determined to support London and Londoners – well, that's what they told me. We were Christmas shopping. My parents took me into a big toy store along Regent Street. Look, there it is."

She pointed to the huge toy shop 'Hamleys'.

"And did you enjoy the experience, Miss Trevillick?"

Laura was surprised on two counts by Mr Millar. First, by his choice of wall decoration and second, by his unusual, if not obsessive, line of questioning. She had expected something more intimidating, more oppressive. She thought carefully before answering.

"I didn't like the crowds of people so much, but I felt quite safe with my parents and of course the shops were great."

Mr Millar sat down and stared at Laura, hungrily, like a wolf, eagerly anticipating a juicy meal of fresh, free-range, live chicken. There was a touch of awe in his voice.

"Tell me what you bought in those shops." He saw her hesitate. "Please, Miss Trevillick."

Laura sat and pondered for a moment, trying hard to remember.

"Well, I know my parents bought lots of presents for friends and family – things like soap and perfumes, books, cards, you know, the usual things."

"But that's just it. I don't know. That's why I'm asking you! What did you buy?"

"I bought sketching pads, pencils, paints, an electronic game, a lovely fluffy teddy bear, it's still in my bedroom," she faltered for a moment. "I think. And loads of books – I love reading… and sketching of course, which reminds me, do you know where my sketch book is?"

Laura realised almost immediately that she had made a mistake in asking this question. Mr Millar's rapturous gaze dissolved and was replaced once again by suspicion.

"What do you want that for? Anxious to get away again are you?"

He saw her flinch and stood up abruptly, moving forward to lean down towards her, his face almost level with her own.

"Oh yes, Miss Trevillick, I'm not as easily taken in as those others. I know you left our world and then came rushing back, anxious to retrieve your precious sketchbook. And now you want it so that you can flit off again. … Believe me; I know your little game."

His hand stretched out and a soft, rather flabby finger brushed against her cheek. Instinctively she stiffened. Mr Millar grinned unpleasantly.

"Such soft skin, such innocence. The young time traveller who manages to fool all the scientists with her sweet youth."

Suddenly he drew his hand back and slapped Laura's face. She gasped and raised her hands defensively. Angry tears bled from her eyes. Mr Millar sneered.

"You don't fool me, not for one single second."

"There's nothing I can tell you," said Laura defiantly and fairly truthfully. "I don't know how I got here…. I don't know why it's such a big deal. I haven't hurt anyone and I haven't got anything you want."

"Ah but my dear Miss Trevillick, that is precisely where you are wrong. You have something very precious indeed."

Laura was genuinely puzzled.

"What's that then?"

"Don't you know? Have you really no idea of what life is like here for someone like me? For someone with my capabilities?"

In response to her shaking head he grasped her wrist and pulled her upright.

"Come with me then, and I'll show you."

Still holding her wrist tightly he led her through his office, pressed a wall panel and entered an elevator as the door slid open. There was no apparent movement, but as Mr Millar's eyes were staring upwards Laura imagined that that was the direction in which they were moving. The journey seemed longer than the others that she had experienced recently, but then, at last, the panel was sliding open. The room they entered was empty but there were heavily shaded windows all round. Laura wondered why she had been brought to this odd location.

"This is a viewing tower, Miss Trevillick. From here you will see what it is that I loathe seeing every day of my life. Here put these on."

Mr Millar handed her some shaded goggles.

"You must keep these on," he said. "They are viewing spectacles, specially designed to protect the human eye from the sun's harmful rays. Do not remove them until I tell you."

They both donned the special glasses. When he was satisfied that Laura's were properly positioned, Mr Millar pressed a hand against the wall and the windows cleared. The room lit up and they seemed almost engulfed in fire.

"Don't worry; we're shielded by the protective glass." He walked to one of the windows. "Come here then, quickly. We're very high up here; you can see for many kilometres all around here. Now, have a look and tell me what you can see."

Laura stared in fascination. From her high vantage point she could indeed see over a huge distance. She tried to remember where she was – Bodmin City State.

'Well, if that's so,' she thought. 'I ought to see as far as Land's End, and maybe even up to Exeter in the other direction.'

But on all four sides of the room she could make out nothing but water. It almost reminded her of the view from the top of St Michael's Mount, except that, there, you could, at least, see the mainland of Marazion and Penzance. She tried to look straight down and could just make out the train that she now realised circled round and round the city state. And then it stopped, as she herself had seen only …. yesterday?

"Look," she cried. "There are people getting off. Where have they come from?"

Mr Millar laughed without any trace of humour. It was more of a bitter cackle.

"Oh yes from a distance they look a little like people I suppose; but close up you can tell that they are just holograms."

Laura was stunned. "Holograms!"

Mr Millar nodded.

"Yes, holograms. One of Computer's little attempts to make us feel more normal. A train that stops and allows people to get off and walk to BCS. Very

65

cleverly done. But as I said, they're only holograms, and even though no one ever takes any notice of them any more, Computer persists in running this utterly useless program."

There was a strong element of contempt in his voice as he said this, which he tried, unsuccessfully to hide.

"Enough of that. Look, look all over. What do you see? Tell me."

Laura looked again, curious, in spite of her loathing for her enforced companion. At first all she could see was water, on all sides and then, in the distance, she could just make out a light blinking, on and off, almost invisible in the bright sunlight. She told Mr Millar what she had seen. She could not make out his eyes, but from the droop in his shoulders he was clearly affected.

"Ah yes, the light. That is coming from Exeter City State – a once thriving community, just like this one."

"Once..?"

"Yes, exactly. Once," Mr Millar's voice hissed. "Once upon a time there was another city state here in the south west, its people in constant communication with us. Once..." he giggled and slumped to the floor. He pressed a wall panel and the windows shaded over. He removed his goggles. Laura followed suit. She was shocked to see how grey and old his face now seemed.

"A once thriving community, just like ours. Alas, not any more."

"What happened?"

"What happened? We're not quite sure; but somehow the structure of the city was breached, the water got in, and that was the end. Many of the inhabitants drowned. Some survived, but whether the water contaminated the supply system or whether their Computer failed we don't know, nor can we ever be sure. After a while we ceased to hear anything."

"But couldn't you have mounted a rescue operation?"

Mr Millar gave Laura a withering look.

"You are so judgemental aren't you, child from the past? Each city state is controlled by its own Computer. We do not have the facilities to implement rescues. If there is a breach, then the citizens have to cope as best they can."

"But where did all this water come from anyway?"

Mr Millar turned his gaze on Laura. There was a look there of disdain, of contempt almost.

"Did you ever hear of Global warming, Miss Trevillick?"

Laura nodded but said nothing.

"Hmm, well, that is something at least. Throughout the latter part of the twentieth century and through most of the twenty first and twenty second centuries, scientists continued to warn successive governments of the dangers of the over use of fossil fuels. Meanwhile other governments tested nuclear weapons; others fought 'dirty' wars. Within an alarmingly short space of time, a few hundred years, the polar ice caps melted, sea levels all over the world rose to unprecedented heights, the ozone layer became perilously thin and even disappeared altogether in places and gradually more and more land became flooded. People fought for land once more. Millions died from war, famine, neglect. Scientists built computers to control what was left of Earth's resources. That's what we have now, a few isolated city states, surrounded by water, with a steadily diminishing population."

"Why is it 'diminishing'?" asked Laura, interested now.

"Pro-creation has taken a bit of a nose-dive somehow. Resources are no longer guaranteed for life, for ever. One day the frozen embryos will run out; plus there's the compulsory euthanasia."

"The what?"

"Compulsory Euthanasia…" repeated Mr Millar. "At the age of 60, instead of receiving a pension, you get the push!"

He started laughing then, a hysterical, harsh, barking noise.

"But that's terrible," said Laura.

"Exactly; terrible is a good word for it Miss Trevillick. And when you are over the age of 55, as I am, it becomes more and more terrible with each passing year. Which is where you come into my life, my dear Miss Trevillick."

"Me?" Laura was mystified. "What? You want me to go back and try to change things? Is that it? Well, of course, I'll do my best, but I don't know if I'll be able to make much of a difference…..I suppose I could join the Green Party or become a 'Friend of the Earth', but even so…"

His mirthless laughter interrupted her long speech.

"You still haven't got it have you? But then you are young and do not have any concept of what I am talking about. There is no way you will be able to change the course of history. Now listen carefully. You are my escape plan, pure and simple; you, Miss Laura

Trevillick. When you return to your own time, I shall be coming with you!"

Chapter 14

Laura shuddered. The thought of allowing Mr Millar to accompany her was thoroughly oppressive and repulsive. As if reading her thoughts Mr Millar was quick to add:

"Oh but you need not worry me. Oh no! Once I am through I won't be a burden, you may rest assured on that. I shall make my way to the capital city – someone there will have a use for me. With my knowledge of the future I shall be invaluable … to the right people. My worth will be very quickly recognised and I will have riches heaped upon me. More importantly, I will be able to live beyond my sixtieth birthday!"

He grabbed her wrists again, tightly.

"You'll be saving my life. You see that don't you?"

Laura tried to pull away, leaning as far away from Mr Millar as possible.

"I don't even know how to get back," she screamed at him. "And even if I did, I'm not sure you'd be able to come back with me, or even be there if the opportunity ever arises again."

Laura glared at her assailant. There was a wild yearning in his eyes, a kind of madness.

"Don't you worry about that Miss Trevillick; I intend to stay with you until we make good our escape."

With this ghastly thought plaguing her, Laura made a desperate effort to escape the hands which clasped her wrists. Mr Millar grinned at her efforts.

"Please don't struggle; we must stick to……"

Just then there was a loud 'hoot', the walls flashed green and yellow and a small panel in the floor slid open.

"What the......" began Mr Millar, turning his head and relaxing the tension on Laura's wrists. That was all she needed. Without hesitation she pulled her arms back sharply, freed her wrists, sped across the floor and dived through the opening.

"NOOOOooooo!..." called Mr Millar. "THAT'S THE EUTHANASIA CHUTE!"

Laura just caught the tail end of his desperate shout. She had little time to take in the horror of her situation however, as she was falling at a considerable speed in what appeared to be a bottomless shaft. She could not make out the bottom, so deep did it appear. She tried spreading out her arms and legs – she had seen television pictures of sky divers doing this – 'I must not panic,' she thought. As she continued falling at a steadily increasing rate, the arms and legs not slowing her at all, she could make out bodies falling or flinging themselves from openings in the shaft. They were all descending to their deaths! At this point Laura could not help herself. She screamed, good and loud!

For a moment or two, or maybe even longer, she must have lost consciousness and then suddenly she was wide awake and falling at a much slower rate. Two older people were floating down alongside her; a man and a woman.

"Hello," said the man in a surprised voice. "You don't look old enough to be here."

"I'm not," shouted Laura. "It's a mistake. I jumped through by accident."

"Oh dear, oh dear," remarked the woman. "You know what they say about accidents, don't you?"

"No, I've no idea. What do they say about accidents?"

"If you're not careful they can lead to serious injuries."

The two sixty year olds evidently found this highly amusing and laughed, almost hysterically.

"I don't see that there is anything to laugh about," said Laura, realising that she sounded just like her maths teacher, Mrs Elliot.

"Better to laugh in the face of death, than to whimper with self pity," came the devastating reply. Laura thought she would have to try to remember that if she ever had the opportunity to use it, which, in the present situation, seemed unlikely. She lowered her eyes and looked down once again. That proved a mistake. She began to feel giddy and sick and her legs started to go higher than her head.

"Help!" she cried feebly.

The man and the woman each grasped her hands and steadied her so that they were, indeed, flying as a threesome.

"Best not to look down," said the man. "There's a heck of a long way to go."

The woman looked at Laura.

"My name's Vera," she said. "And this is my very good friend David."

"Pleased to meet you. I'm Laura."

"I don't want to appear rude, but I don't remember seeing you before. Are you from round here?"

"I was born locally, but this my first visit to Bodmin City State."

"That's a pity," said David.

"Why?"

"Well, it looks like it could also be your last visit."

Once again Vera and David began to laugh in their own inimitable fashion. Laura was about to reply when something or someone grabbed her ankles. She screamed.

"It's alright Laura," called a familiar voice. "It's me Samantha. Don't worry; we'll have you back in no time. May I ask you, David and Vera, if you'd mind letting go of Laura's hands please?"

The man and the woman looked at one another.

"I suppose we ought to," said David. "Goodbye dear, it has been so nice to meet you."

Laura felt her hands being gently released. She watched as the pair began to spiral and descend below her. As she watched, she saw the couple draw themselves closer together and kiss. Laura was so moved, she began to weep. Slowly, slowly she was hauled back to safety.

Chapter 15

Safely inside, Laura gave full vent to her tears. Detective Flick did her best to provide a comforting hug.

"Come on now," she said. "You're safe here with us."

"It's not me I'm crying for," sobbed Laura. "It's all those sixty year olds, floating down to, to …."

She continued her crying while Doctors Sternman and Chang looked on in an embarrassed silence.

When Laura at last calmed down she was led into a room where they all sat down together. She was asked if she required anything, but shook her head. Finally, unable to bear the silence any longer she said

"How did you know where to rescue me?"

Dr Sternman cleared his throat.

"Most residents know about the signals for the Euthanasia Chute, but incidents very occasionally do occur. The rate of descent can be interrupted so that we can implement a rescue. There was never any real danger that you would become an innocent victim."

"How did you know I was in the Chute?"

"Every citizen of BCS has a micro chip implanted at birth. It enables each person to find his or her way round and to make full use of all the facilities available. Then, at age 60, it becomes activated and leads the citizens to voluntarily enter the chute. The chip cuts off the normal fear mechanism so that our senior citizens' last moments are tranquil and peaceful. If an inactivated chip, or, as in your case, a non-chipped organism, enters then Computer automatically registers the anomaly and informs the appropriate persons. In this instance you were identified and so we were the informed group, hence your safe retrieval."

Laura stared at Dr Sternman. His explanation was so cool and matter-of-fact. Her gaze swept across to Dr Chang and finally settled on Samantha Flick.

"I don't understand," said Laura.

"What don't you understand?" asked Samantha.

"Why do people have to go in the Euthanasia Chute in the first place? It seems so cruel, so heartless. You've all been very kind to me, and yet, you seem not to notice people leaping to …."

She could not bring herself to say anymore as tears welled up in her eyes again. There was silence for a while, apart from Laura's gulps and sniffs. When she had dried her eyes she looked directly at Dr Sternman.

"Well?" she asked.

He moved his hanging chair so that he could sit beside her.

"You mustn't think that because we appear not to take any notice or to visibly grieve, that we are heartless…, but the fact is that this is the tradition here. This ceremony has been taking place for hundreds of years. It was developed so that others might live…."

He paused to study Laura's face. She still looked unconvinced.

"Perhaps it would be as well if Detective Flick showed you round some of our facilities; that may give you some idea of our situation here. What do you think?"

Laura sniffed and nodded.

"Come along then Laura," said Samantha in a no-nonsense fashion. "We'll start at the bottom and work our way up. I hope you've got plenty of time."

'Time,' thought Laura. 'I wonder how much time I've got.' She followed Samantha through another series of walks and elevator rides. On one of the elevator journeys Samantha asked Laura if Mr Millar had been with her when she 'accidentally' fell into the chute.

"Why do you ask?"

Samantha smiled. "Well, I am supposed to be a detective, and it is strange that Mr Millar hasn't been seen since that incident."

"Did you know that he'd come to see me this morning; called to collect me, straight from my room."

"He had informed us that he needed to speak with you urgently, saying it had to do with City state security."

"And you believed him!" Laura spluttered.

"Shouldn't we have?"

Laura was so silent that Samantha felt prompted to ask another question.

"You're not telling me that he pushed you into the chute?"

"No, of course not. I jumped of my own free will."

"Whatever for?"

"You're the detective, work it out."

Just then the elevator door opened and they stepped out onto a walk-way overlooking several rows of babies, all of whom seemed to be sleeping. Laura stared, quite stunned by the sight. She had never seen this many babies all sleeping in one place in her entire life.

"You're very privileged Laura."

"Why?"

"Not many people get to witness this sight – the next generation of BCS citizens. Beautiful, aren't they?"

"But where have they all come from? Where are their mothers?"

Samantha gazed down thoughtfully and sighed.

"I suppose all the present citizens of BCS are their parents. We get to care for them as they grow up."

"But don't they have real mothers?"

Samantha looked at Laura almost shyly.

"Do you have a mother, in your own time?" she asked.

"Of course, she's …... she's lovely."

Laura bent her head to hide the tears which were threatening to overwhelm her again. Samantha pursed her lips together.

"You're very lucky then. This is how I was born, one of fifty babies; we're produced every twenty years or so."

Laura was horrified.

"Produced? What do you mean 'produced'?"

"We're grown – from frozen eggs. Mass produced. In an orderly fashion. Progress is wonderful isn't it?"

"Who looks after them all?"

"They're all monitored by Computer, but a team of nurses is on hand at all times."

"So the nurses look after any babies that are unwell?"

"They're never unwell."

Laura looked perplexed.

"But babies are always unwell; you know, colds, sniffles, coughs, that sort of thing."

"Babies here do not get ill. All childhood diseases have been eliminated. Any defective eggs are destroyed. Not that we have many of those left."

"Goodness, it sounds very clinical."

"Listen to me Laura. In the world in which we live now we have to be clinical; we cannot afford to have any epidemics within the city state. That's why you were scanned when you first entered. Any unknown or unwanted microbes would have been dealt with then – otherwise you could have wiped us all out." Seeing Laura's look of horror, Samantha quickly added: "Come on, you're fine now, let's carry on with our tour."

The babies were behind a glass screen, or, at least, what appeared to be a glass screen. For all Laura knew it could have been made of a product entirely unknown in the twenty first century. Samantha continued walking. She went past a laboratory where a few people were working.

"What's going on here?" Laura's curiosity was going at full throttle now!

"Just routine testing. We have other areas where scientists work on such things as desalination – to help maintain our fresh water supplies; engineers who keep an eye on the solar powered generators, food scientist. All those are on these lower levels."

"Are there any schools for children?"

"No, all education is conducted by Computer. Through Computer you may go as far as your capabilities allow."

"And what about churches and God and worship – do you have anything like that here?"

Samantha looked at her almost indignantly.

"We have no use for such things here. Computer provides for us and we are satisfied. There is no need for churches or worship."

Laura thought that she'd better change the subject quickly.

"How low down are we now then?"

"We're about four kilometres below the current level of the sea."

"But the air still feels good down here, there's no smell at all."

"Of course not. Air is still extracted from outside, but it is cleaned and purified and distributed throughout the City State."

"And that's all controlled by Computer?"

"Yes, but the scientists check the levels from time to time."

Something was nagging at Laura's brain – but she was almost afraid to ask the question. Nevertheless, she could not leave it unspoken.

"What would happen if Computer ever stopped working?"

Samantha gasped, genuinely shocked.

"Such a thing would be unthinkable," she said and walked on resolutely. In her own way Laura was also shocked. Back in her own time of 2009, computers were always crashing; even government departments lost huge sums of money because expensive programs failed. If it was 'unthinkable', that could mean only one thing. If Computer did ever fail, it would mean the end for Bodmin City State.

Chapter 16

Laura ran to catch up. Samantha was striding ahead resolutely, almost ignoring her. "Wait Sam," she called. Samantha paused and waited.

"I'm sorry," said Laura when she finally caught up. "I didn't mean to upset you."

"I'm sorry too. We get a bit sensitive about certain things. You just touched a few raw nerves. No harm done. Now, is there anything else you'd like to know?"

"Yes, loads! For example, in my time, NASA was talking about landing humans on Mars, exploring the stars and so on. What happened to all that?"

Samantha grinned, pleased to move on to safer territory.

"I'll show you. Come on this way."

She walked off briskly with Laura hurrying to keep up. They passed through several sliding doors and took the elevator up to the next floor.

"Here we are."

Laura looked round helplessly.

"That's the trouble with this place. Everywhere looks exactly the same. Where are we?"

"I think you'll enjoy this," said Samantha, grinning again like a Cheshire cat. "Plus it will be very informative."

She placed her hand on the wall in front and they entered a darkened room. Laura could just make out a group of seats with what looked like seat belts attached.

"This looks a bit ominous," suggested Laura.

"Not at all. It's the Kinetic Environment Studio – KES for short. We come here for a mixture of education and entertainment. Take a seat."

Laura did so and Samantha sat alongside her.

"What we'll see and experience is an amalgam of some of the more important actual manned space missions which have taken place over time. You will need to put on your seat belt – it will adjust to your body mass automatically. If it gets too much for you all you have to do is shout 'STOP'. OK?"

"It sounds as if it's going to be scary."

"It is! But it's also tremendously adventurous. I've experienced it on several occasions."

"And you don't mind sitting through it again?"

"I love it! I seem to encounter something new each time I sit here. There are lots of other presentations too, mostly educational. But Computer makes you feel as if you're really there. You'll see."

The sliding door opened and several more people entered and took seats. They smiled and waved at Samantha and nodded politely at Laura.

"Is this a regular showing?" whispered Laura. "Or are they here just coincidentally?"

"Once the area is entered, others are automatically informed that a showing is about to take place. Anyone who has the time, and who wants to, can then come along."

"But, supposing they don't want to watch what we're going to see?"

"Don't worry. The presentations are so good, that it doesn't matter. Now, as the first here I can choose what we are all going to experience. Are you ready?"

Laura nodded, a little nervously, wondering quite what she was letting herself in for.

"Computer," called Samantha. "Programme 13, Manned Space Missions. Thank You."

Almost immediately headsets descended. Laura watched carefully as Samantha and the other occupants fitted the headsets and followed suit when Samantha nodded at her to do the same.

"Now remember," said Samantha, "Just relax and be ready."

The room darkened as a visor slipped down over Laura's face.

'10, 9, 8, 7, 6, 5, 4, 3, 2, 1   We Have Lift Off!'

Astonishingly, Laura felt herself rising; she turned her head and saw, not Samantha, but two astronauts. She realised this was some kind of simulation, but it was incredibly realistic. There were even G-forces pressing down on her. Just when she thought she was going to stop breathing altogether, there was a sudden release of all pressure and a feeling of lightness in her limbs. Through a porthole she could see Earth. Then a voice said 'Neil and Buzz, would you take your position in the Lunar Module,' and she and another astronaut were moving as instructed, and taking up station in the rather cramped quarters of the module. Her fellow astronaut looked at her. 'Isn't this beautiful Buzz,' he said. 'We're now orbiting the moon – soon we'll be separating and flying down to the surface – the first men to land on the moon.'

Laura found it difficult to believe what she was experiencing; even when she heard the unforgettable 'The Eagle has landed – The Eagle has landed!' When that was followed by some bounding steps on what was obviously the surface of the moon, she knew it was for real. Incredibly, she found herself saying 'That's one small step for a man, a giant leap for mankind.'

The presentation continued in the same vein with adventures on Apollo's 15 and 16 and fun in the Lunar Rover; with the Apollo 17's mission and the last lunar landing of the 20th century. She endured life on board Skylab 4 in 1973 and took part in a number of Space Shuttle flights, including the disastrous Challenger flight on 28th January 1986 which made her weep bucket-loads of tears. She joined Dennis Tito as the first private space tourist, thus saving herself several million pounds. In August 2010, not too far ahead of her own time, she helped to deliver the Kito Japanese Experimental Logistics module to the International Space Station,

The Mars manned expeditions began in 2050 and she was there for the first successful landing, and the second, when a settlement was begun in 2093.

But it was the development of new technology which led to the building of the first star ship which really captured her imagination. Here was the vessel, begun in 2376, which would take humanity to the stars. She participated in all the test runs and felt the certainty that this would be the way forward for the entire Human race.

At that point the visor was raised, and she realised the presentation was at an end. Laura was both exhilarated and exhausted, but she felt a sense of triumph. A manned star-ship had left Earth in search of a new homeland. Somewhere, in an unknown star system, a thriving community might well have established itself.

83

Her sense of euphoria subsided as she realised that she must have been sweating copious amounts of fluid – her mouth was dry and her clothes were decidedly sticky. Her look, as she rose from her chair must have said it all – Samantha laughed.

"Now you know how the astronauts must have felt in their suits."

She took Laura to a section of the wall which opened up as they approached – others were doing the same.

"Pop in there," said Samantha. "It's a revitalising room, especially for such occasions."

Gently she propelled Laura into a booth. The door slid closed and after a few seconds a rush of warm air swept through. Laura found this quite pleasing at first, but this was swiftly followed by a douche of hot steamy water which left her dripping, clothes and all! Finally another blast of warm air rushed through and was maintained until Laura, together with her clothes, was thoroughly dry once again. The door slid open and she met Samantha stepping out of her booth. They both laughed at the sight of the other's frizzed up hair.

"Come on, I'll treat you to a drink."

Laura followed Samantha into an adjoining room. She was pleasantly surprised to see that it almost resembled a café; there were chairs and tables and a few people from the audience were already there drinking and chatting. There was no bar though. Samantha went over to an oblong recess in the wall, placed her hand against it and tapped twice. Two small beakers appeared which she brought over the table at which Laura had sat down.

"Computer is great," said Samantha raising her cup. Laura lifted her own cup and replied with "Cheers!"

"That sounds like a very old fashioned remark; what does it mean?"

Laura shook her head, not quite knowing what to make of this question.

"I don't know really, I've never thought about it. It's just something we say to each other if we're having a drink together."

"We know what we mean." Samantha was quite decisive. "Without Computer, we would not survive; so to us, the expression 'Computer is Great' really means something."

"OK then," said Laura, not wishing to offend, but still thinking 'cheers'. "Computer is great!"

She raised her cup and sipped. If she was expecting coffee, tea or hot chocolate then she was disappointed. The beverage was probably very good for you, she thought, but tasted fairly neutral – if anything, veering towards something like a beef or vegetable extract. Samantha saw the effects on her face.

"It's a very nutritious drink," she insisted. "It will replace the energy you lost during your flights into space."

"Thanks, I'm sure it's doing me the world of good." Laura tried hard not to sound sarcastic. She decided to change the subject. "Tell me, that final part of the presentation that we saw, about the star ship. Was that a successful flight? Why didn't we experience any more of the journey?"

Samantha shrugged her shoulders.

85

"Who knows? Computer decides what is shown. We do know that the flight took place several hundred years ago now. The journey itself was going to take many, many years. It may even still be going on, searching for that elusive planet. Unfortunately the survival of the Earth itself at that time was in doubt, so the NASA scientists rushed the Star Ship program through very quickly. We do know that the ship safely passed through our own solar system....but after that...nothing. Now, today, we have no means of tracking or finding such a craft. I really hope though, that they found what they were looking for and have successfully colonised a new world."

"Was that the only star ship to be built?"

"No! Two more were almost ready."

"Well! What happened to them?"

"There was some kind of explosion. But since both ships were severely damaged, and since they were in different locations it was deemed to be an act of war."

Laura was almost afraid to ask the next question. She took a deep breath.

"So, what happened then?"

There was a shrug of the shoulders which Laura now recognised as a typical Samantha move.

"The usual. The men in charge took the decision to fire rockets, there were battles at sea and on land, but in the end nobody benefited because the sea water only started rising higher. That's when our ancestors began designing and building separate city states in the high places."

Laura swallowed the rest of her drink without noticing the taste any longer. 'So that was it,' she thought. 'War, global warming, floods – everything that had been forecast by scientists for years, and the result: humanity brought to its knees and forced to live inside tin boxes.'

"It's a rather bleak outlook, isn't it?" she said, rather mournfully.

Samantha was silent for a while.

"This is the only life I've ever known. I'm different to you. I'm a person of this world. I'm content with what I have here. It's the only form of existence that I'm aware of. Even if there was another star ship waiting outside, I wouldn't go on it!

"Why not?"

"Because I'm used to my life here. Most people know their place if you like. Also, we're grateful to Computer. It keeps us alive – it maintains this city state; it regulates the food we eat and the liquids we drink. We are always in good health. Why should we wish to leave?"

"Mr Millar wants to leave."

Laura waited to see what effect this statement would have. There was quite a long pause before Samantha finally asked: "How do you know this?"

"He told me so. He wants to leave BCS and follow me into my own time."

"And how does he propose to do this?"

Now it was Laura's turn to shrug her shoulders.

"I think his intention was to stick with me until a way appeared for me to return."

"So that's why you jumped into the chute!"

Laura blushed.

"I'm sorry," was all she could think to say.

Samantha smiled sympathetically.

"Don't be silly – it wasn't your fault. You must have been desperate to do something like that. Did he threaten you?"

"He didn't exactly threaten me, but…"

"Yes?"

"Well, he was kind of frightening, you know. He seemed so determined that I would be able to help him to …leave…I suppose."

"I'll see that he does not threaten you again." Samantha took a small device from her uniform. "Computer – can you tell me the location of Mr Millar?"

The reply came back quickly.

'Mr Millar does not appear to be inside BCS.' There was another short pause. 'Records show that Mr Millar took a protection suit and other supplies and left the confines of City State. It is likely therefore that he is on an external expedition.'

"Thank you Computer." Samantha returned the device. "Hmmm, interesting."

Laura thought it was a lot more than just 'interesting'!

"Is he allowed to do that?"

"Oh yes, it is perfectly legitimate for him to leave the city and go on a reconnaissance – he has informed us in the past that it is part of his job as head of security. What good it has ever done I don't know."

"Maybe it's his way of … just…escaping from the city from time to time."

"But where can he go? There's nothing out there except uncomfortable heat and water, water everywhere – It wouldn't even take him that long to walk around the island."

"Don't other people sometimes go out?"

"No, it is not necessary." Samantha's tone was brusque. After a moment she relaxed. "I don't suppose he can come to any harm out there; he does have protective clothing on at least."

"When you talk about 'harm' – do you mean actual bodily harm to himself, or physical harm to the city?"

Samantha looked shocked.

"Harm to the city state! Why that would be unthinkable, unbelievable – it would be the act of a mad ….."

She stared at Laura, horror dawning on her face: "But then, if he's so desperate that he frightened you, maybe he is a little mad. Quickly," she stood up. "We must get back to my office as quickly as possible."

Laura followed her as she ran across to an elevator. Once inside Samantha used her device to contact Doug.

"Hi Doug, get protection suits ready for us. We must locate Mr Millar – he's outside and I believe in danger of doing something foolish. Contact Dr Sternman. I'll be with you very shortly."

"You're really worried, aren't you?" said Laura.

Samantha nodded.

"But why, what harm can he do?"

"I'm not sure, but if he's in an odd state of mind he could be dangerous – he could damage the solar panels and interfere with our energy supplies; he could de-rail the train…"

"What? Why would that be dangerous?"

"I'm not sure, I don't know," she was almost shouting. "It might just do enough damage to cause a breach in the sea wall defences…Whatever he's planning, we've got to get out there and stop him before he gets the chance."

The elevator door slid open and they ran along the corridor until they reached another elevator.

"This one will take us directly to our offices."

And soon enough they were with Doug who had prepared two suits.

"Is there one for me?" asked Laura.

"And why would you need one, young lady?" said Doug, emphasising the word 'young'.

"Maybe I can help persuade Mr Millar to come in."

Doug looked at his fellow officer who was just getting into her suit.

"Sure," she said. "You might be able to help, but don't try to interfere with anything we do, understood?"

"Understood!"

"Sounds crazy to me," said Doug. "But I'll try and find you a suit that fits your slim frame."

He ran off. Samantha, meanwhile, had finished dressing. She looked as if she was about to go scuba diving; there was even complete head covering with mask and small oxygen bottle. She flipped open her mask.

"Why do you have an oxygen tank?" asked Laura.

"That's just a precaution. We live so much indoors now that our skin is very sensitive. Similarly, the 'hot air' outside could damage our lungs if we breathed in too much, so 'safety first' is always our aim on such ventures. Ah, look here comes Doug."

It did not take long for Laura to get sorted into her suit and she was surprised to find how well she could move about with it in place. She soon picked up the controls which would enable her to adjust the oxygen flow if necessary and also allow her to communicate more easily with her companions.

"Right," said Doug. "This should be exciting. Let's go!"

Chapter 17

They rode the elevator together – a strangely incongruous trio of non-aquatic frog persons – and then went along a passageway. This brought them into a small block alongside the city entrance. A wall slid open for them, let them out, and then slid shut. When Laura looked back the wall looked completely seamless. Samantha had another device in her hand, which, now they were in the open, she was able to activate.

"It's a kind of homing device," she explained to Laura. "It will help us to locate Mr Millar. All the suits are designed this way for emergency purposes, though I've not had to use one for a long time."

"Will Mr Millar know we're using this to find him?"

"He will probably expect us to come looking for him anyway, so make sure you keep close to us."

"Come on, come on you two, let's get going," said Doug, a little impatiently.

They set off, retracing the steps that Laura herself had taken only the day before. Ahead they could see the train coming to a halt. As before, business-like figures stepped off the train and came towards them, only now, as they drew nearer, Laura realised that she could actually see through them, that they were, indeed, no more than cleverly constructed holograms.

"The train seems OK," said Doug. "Shall we get on and go round the Island that way?"

"Might be a bit quicker," said Samantha. "The 'scope shows he's round the far side. Come on let's get on before it moves off."

They sprinted now and jumped on to the train. Laura was pleasantly surprised at how comfortable she continued to feel inside her suit. She was about to sit down when Doug held her back. "Don't bother," he said. "We're not going that far."

She looked out of the train windows and saw the sea, close by, with waves gently lapping against a sea defence wall. It all looked almost idyllic and peaceful; she wondered if it would remain so.

The train slowed down slightly as it began to curve into the bend, round the city.

"Get ready to jump off when I say," called Samantha. "Don't worry about your suit Laura, it's very tough."

Laura had never in her life jumped from any moving vehicle, except perhaps her old bicycle, so she was more worried about her own self, not the suit!

"NOW!" called Samantha.

All three of them jumped together; the two detectives landed on their feet while Laura would have tumbled in an undignified heap had not Doug caught her arm and held her upright.

"Thanks," she managed to croak.

The train, meanwhile, continued on its journey, leaving them behind to whatever fate had in store.

"Are you ok?" asked Samantha.

In reply, Laura confirmed that she was perfectly fine, thank you, and very comfortable in her suit.

"These suits, or ones very much like them, were used on the star ships – they might still be in use somewhere out there." Samantha's voice was wistful and Laura wondered if she was lonely, living in the closed-in environment of a city state. She and Samantha stood squinting, even with the protective goggles, into the vast blue sky, trying to imagine what lay out there, many light years away.

"Come on you two," called Doug from some distance. "I think I can see him."

The two females turned then and clambered over the rocky surface.

"Look there he is," shouted Doug. "He's burying something by the railway line. Come on."

While they were hurrying towards Mr Millar, Laura caught hold of Samantha's arm.

"What will you do with Mr Millar?" she asked.

"We'll escort him back with us, that's all."

"And then what?"

"Well, Dr Sternman and Dr Chang may have to do some analysis, and then help him correct any defects."

Laura was not convinced that this would do the trick, but she kept these thoughts to herself. By now they had reached Doug who was standing quite still. He was staring at another suited figure that could only be Mr Millar; the security chief was holding what looked like a gun and pointing it straight at Doug.

Chapter 18

"Who's there?" called Mr Millar through their headsets. "No doubt the dedicated detectives, Flick and Connors – but who's that with you? Not young Laura surely? Why that's excellent, and how considerate of you to bring her to me."

Doug stepped forward one pace. Mr Millar turned the gun towards a large rock, activated the firing mechanism and the rock shattered, spraying them with debris.

"I hope that persuades you to come no further. I would have no hesitation in using this on any one of you two detectives."

Samantha now stood alongside Doug. She carefully manoeuvred Laura so that she was standing behind them.

"Mr Millar," she called. "You have an illegal weapon. Owning and using such an implement has been banned for over two hundred years. Please place it on the ground and prepare to be escorted back to BCS,"

Mr Millar's sardonic laugh rang in their ears, a harsh reminder of his unbalanced mind.

"Brave words Detective Flick, but you don't really expect me to obey you now, do you? After all, I am the senior representative here." He laughed again, delighted at his own idea of a joke. The two detectives turned their backs and spoke quietly to Laura.

"You must keep behind us at all times Laura," said Samantha.

"And if he starts firing that thing," went on Doug "lie down as flat as you can."

"But what is it?" asked Laura, peering anxiously round at the deranged man.

Doug shook his head.

"It's some horror that he's either found or made himself."

Laura, who had surprisingly enjoyed a number of old, often repeated westerns tossed the situation round her head.

"Well, can't you draw your own weapons and disarm him or something?"

Samantha and Doug looked at one another and then turned back to stare at Laura, and she felt that, even with their masks on, they were looking at her rather dismissively.

"What? What is it?" she asked anxiously.

"Shall I tell her?" said Doug.

Samantha nodded.

"The thing is, Laura, we don't have any weapons. There haven't been weapons allowed in BCS for a very long time. Nobody, not even the head of security is supposed to be in possession of a weapon."

"So, can you do anything?"

"Maybe," said Doug. "I'm going to count to three and then we're all going to dive for cover and Sam and I will activate the chip immobiliser."

"The chip is the device we all have implanted at birth. As detectives we are the only people entrusted with immobilisers – if we aim these at Mr Millar, he will become temporarily paralysed and we can disarm him. Ready?"

Laura, who felt that this was just like a western, nodded.

"Right, one, two, three – go!"

They dived down flat and Samantha and Doug pressed pads on their suits. Mr Millar staggered forward, and then lowered his head and his weapon. Doug leapt up.

"Come on Sam," he called. "We can get him now."

"No wait," shouted Samantha, but Doug was already on his way over. Laura and Samantha were just getting to their feet when they heard an unpleasant cackling. Mr Millar lifted his head, raised his weapon and fired. Doug had no chance. The girls screamed out "NO!" but it was too late and Laura covered her eyes and wept.

"That's the trouble with our esteemed police force," yelled Mr Millar. "It places too much reliance on technology. I deactivated my own chip months ago! And now see the result. The detective department is reduced to half a force!"

Through her tears Laura looked at Samantha.

"Half.... What's he mean? Half a force?"

Samantha lowered her head on the ground. "There are,.." she choked for a moment. "There were, just the two of us."

"A police force of just two?" Laura couldn't quite believe what she was hearing.

"Two?" she repeated.

"There's never any crime here, we don't need a large force. Each department in BCS has just two people."

Laura felt terrible. She hadn't known. Poor Samantha, she thought, it must be like losing a brother.

Mr Millar, meanwhile, was approaching them. He made his way carefully over the ground where Doug had last been seen. He stopped a short distance from Samantha and Laura, lowered the weapon and removed something from a pocket. He held it up above his head.

"Now then Miss Flick, you are the detective here – would you like to tell me what I have in my hand?"

Samantha glared at him. "You disgust me!" she screamed.

"Now then, don't let's get personal. Just answer the question."

Samantha took a long, deep breath.

"No doubt you have some dangerous and totally illegal instrument."

Mr Millar tossed it, seemingly carelessly, into the air, but took great care to catch it safely.

"Mmm," he murmured. "That's a bit non-specific. What about you, Miss Trevillick, what do you think it is?"

Laura, who was both an avid reader as well as a film fan, made an educated guess. "Is it some kind of detonating device?"

"Very good; in fact, excellent. You see, detective Flick, our friend Laura from the past is a better detective than you are!" He laughed unfeelingly.

"What is it you want, Millar?"

"Oh dear, not so polite any more. What a pity. Oh well, I'll not waste any more of your terribly precious time. This device, as Miss Trevillick has correctly pointed out, is a detonating mechanism. It has several switches, each of which leads to a different, but nevertheless, potentially destructive spot around the perimeter of BCS."

"Why?" called Samantha. "What do you want?"

"Don't be so obtuse, detective! You know perfectly well what, or rather, who I want. And if she is not given over to me immediately I will puncture holes in both the sea defences and the city walls … and you know what that will mean, don't you? Of course, I can just come over and take her from you – but that would be so messy – again! Just hand her over or it's goodbye BCS."

"But why do you want Laura?"

"Oh I think you know. She will help me to escape from this prison – she is my visitor 'pass'." He laughed humourlessly, then turned nasty again. "Now, what's it to be? You have only a very short time to make up your mind. After that – it's holes in the wall!"

He swaggered back, sure of himself.

"He really is totally unhinged," said Samantha. "How is this possible? No one, to my knowledge, has behaved in this murderous fashion, certainly not in my lifetime. How has Computer let this happen?"

Laura tugged at Samantha's arm.

"Never mind Computer. There's only one thing we can do now, isn't there?"

"What's that?"

"Let him follow me around until I get back to my own world."

"You have no idea what you're saying! Besides the fact that he could create havoc there, or worse still, change the course of our history – there's the impact it will have on you. How long do you think you could stand Mr Millar around you?"

"But maybe that's the point. Maybe the reason we're here now is because of the effect he might have in the past."

Samantha was silent for a moment, clearly weighing up the implications of Laura's remarks. At last she sat up. Mr Millar turned immediately.

"Listen," whispered Samantha. "If we get him back inside, the weapon will become unusable. Computer does not allow such equipment inside BCS. I'm not sure about the detonators though, nor about what the other citizens will think if we bring him back inside."

Laura ignored the last remark.

"So how did he get the weapon – in a shop down the road? Will Computer be able to deal with detonators?"

The lone detective shook her head.

"We will just have to let the wind shake the situation dry." Having made this odd remark to Laura, she then clicked the voice communicator switch. "Listen Millar. Laura has agreed to go with you. You must promise not to harm her."

"I'm glad to see you've come to your senses," he said. "But you need have no fear for Miss Trevillick's safety. I have absolutely no intention of harming her. It's your own self you need to be concerned about. Now then young lady, over here!"

Laura got up and walked across to Mr Millar.

"No tricks," he called, rather unnecessarily. "Now you, get up."

Samantha stood as Laura reached his side.

"Listen carefully Miss Trevillick. I'm sure that Detective Flick has told you that this weapon will not work inside BCS." Laura nodded. "Well that's quite true, but the detonators have a special frequency which will activate the explosive devices I have hidden around the city walls and along the sea defences. So, one slip from you or anyone else and it's 'goodbye' home and 'hello' sea."

They all walked back to the moving path. On the way Mr Millar kept up a continuous stream of conversation detailing how, on his numerous trips outside BCS he had 'brilliantly' constructed the weapon from plans he had discovered while going through old security files; how he had set up the explosive devices 'just in case' he ever needed the opportunity; and how incredibly easy it had been to 'fool' everybody. He showed no remorse for Doug – plainly, in his euphoric state, he had already forgotten him. From the way she walked, with head bowed, Samantha seemed in a state of shock. Looking at the two of them, Laura wondered how the events of the morning would affect the whole community within BCS. She was soon to find out just how extreme their reaction would be.

Chapter 19

When they had returned and removed their suits, Mr Millar discarded his now useless weapon but kept a tight hold on his detonating device. Samantha then led them into a reception area where a large body of people, including Dr Sternman and Dr Chang, was waiting. There was an air of sadness rather than anger and Laura felt very unhappy about being part of the cause. Samantha walked over to the waiting group where she quietly explained what had happened. It was clear from the relatively calm way that the story was received that most of the people there already knew most of the facts; Laura assumed that after they had suited up and left the safety of BCS, cameras had followed their every move. Seeing Doug obliterated must have been devastating. Just thinking about it again made Laura deeply unhappy. Unfortunately, things were about to get even worse.

Dr Sternman stepped forward. He did not look at Mr Millar but spoke directly to Laura.

"Miss Tre..." he began, then hesitated and, after thinking for a moment, continued again. "My dear Laura; because of the dreadful nature of Mr Millar's crimes and because of his determination to use you as a means of escape, we have had to make the unhappy decision to send you both to 'country'. All communication with you will cease. You will not be able to contact Computer unless Computer itself wishes, and all recreational facilities will be barred. Food and shelter, of course, will be provided – we, after all, are not murderers."

Mr Millar grunted, but made no further comment. Laura, however, could not understand what was going on.

"But, Dr Sternman, it seems like you're punishing me. Is that right?" she asked, and when the doctor nodded gravely, said: "But why? I haven't done anything!"

"We recognise that you are innocent of any criminal intent. Nevertheless, your presence here has precipitated these unhappy events. We will ensure that you and your companion have the necessities to sustain life, but our dearest wish, now, is that both of you will succeed in finding a way back to your own world and out of our city."

While Laura was still trying to work out what all this meant, Dr Sternman turned his back on her and slowly walked away. All the other people in the reception area did the same – it was almost as if they were re-enacting some ancient rite. Only Samantha still faced them. She stepped forward slowly and handed Laura a shoulder bag.

"This is yours Laura," she said, her eyes glistening with unwept tears. "I'm so sorry. The council has made its decision; I'm not even allowed to…" She took a deep breath, turned and walked back to the group, the Council, which now proceeded to walk slowly from the room. It wasn't too long before Laura stood there quite alone with only her 'companion', Mr Millar, for company.

A door slid open and Mr Millar took Laura's arm and steered her into the room that was being made available for their exclusive use. The thought of having to remain with Mr Millar until an exit door appeared filled Laura with extreme discomfort. Once they were inside the room and the door had slid shut behind them, she pulled away from him. She walked across to the other side and, to give herself something to do, opened the shoulder bag. Inside was her sketch book with some extra drawing equipment. She knelt down on the floor and hugged it to herself – the one single item that was part of her own world.

A slot opened in one of the silver walls. Mr Millar went over to it.

"How civilised," he declared. "Sent to 'country' but still fed. Good. I need some sustenance after all my superhuman efforts this morning. Here, you'd better eat as well."

He pulled out a tray which held two food bars and two tumblers. Laura waited until he had taken his own supplies before going to collect her rations.

"Do you understand what being sent to 'country' means?" asked Mr Millar.

Laura nodded. "I was unsure at first, but then I understood. In my time we call it being sent to 'Coventry'."

"I suppose if I were a student of the development of language I might be interested – but, quite frankly, my main interest is in leaving this hideous place and visiting a real world, with real people and real events." His eyes bulged at the thought, and for a moment he seemed to Laura like a naughty schoolboy. She opened her sketchbook. Doug's portrait stared at her hauntingly.

"Why did you have to....to kill him?" she asked, not angrily now, but with deep sadness.

"It was a demonstration of my power. These people here have grown soft – they have no ambition, no purpose in life – except to keep BCS ticking over. There's no progress. The sea isn't receding and there's no way of increasing our land mass. Computer tells us when it's day or night. Computer tells us when to go to bed and when to get up in the morning. Computer decides when we're born...and when we die. I cannot believe that I am the only person in two hundred years or more to have challenged that idea. Whereas, your people travel the world, eat exotic foods, explore space – in other words, they are vibrant living beings."

He scurried over to Laura and knelt beside her, ignoring the way she shrank back from him.

"Can you see why I was so desperate to escape? Every fibre in my body was quivering in despair. No wonder so many people willingly enter the Euthanasia Chute!"

"But you killed Doug – senselessly!" repeated Laura.

"One person, that's all! In your time thousands are killed every year – blown up, shot, starved, massacred. I have got what I want with just one fatality!"

"But you were willing to destroy BCS, weren't you?"

Mr Millar shrugged. "Perhaps; but they're practically dead anyway. At least now I've shaken them up a bit; at least now, I've given them something to think about, to become emotional over. One day they may even thank me!"

He got up then, his head held high like some 31st century Brutus, and sat on a seat on the opposite side of the room where he slowly devoured his food bar.

105

"You should eat too Miss Trevillick," he said. "You will need to keep your strength up; we may be here for some time."

Chapter 20

In fact, they were incarcerated for almost a week; the loneliest time of Laura's life. Somehow, the only door which slid aside for them was that leading to the shower and toilet. Whenever Laura used either of these facilities, Mr Millar insisted that she keep talking or singing, so that he would know that she was still in there and had not slipped through, somehow, into her own time. Sleeping was also uncomfortable, as the former head of security would tie a rope from Laura's arm to his own, again, 'just in case'. For Laura, it was the most unpleasant and uncomfortable experience of her young life and, since Computer failed to address them or to allow a change of view, her only distraction was to draw and write incessantly. For his part, Mr Millar paced up and down constantly.

By the sixth day, almost every available space in the sketch book had been utilised and Laura felt sure that she was near to breaking point. Even Mr Millar looked exhausted, his eyes ringed with black, his cheeks hollow. The detonator now lay idle on the floor as if he had forgotten it, and Laura almost felt tempted to casually pick it up in order to flush it down the toilet. Only the 'not knowing' what might happen to them and the danger of accidental detonation had stopped her, but now, she felt, she must do something. She leapt up from her seat, went across to a wall where she thought they might have entered the room originally and banged with both fists on the matt silver which now seemed so oppressive.

"This isn't fair!" she shouted.

Behind her, she heard Mr Millar chuckle.

"Aha, young lady!" he cried. "Now you know how I have felt all these years."

Laura turned and was about to rage and shout at him when she saw, to her great astonishment and relief, that Mr Millar was now leaning back against a door; a real door. The effect clearly showed on her face, for Mr Millar immediately stood upright saying "What is it? What have you seen? A way out?" Then he saw where her eyes were staring and turned. The cry he gave was a cross between a sob and a yell of triumph. He reached for the door handle and tried to turn it. Nothing happened. He looked back at Laura, his hand still on the handle of the door as if afraid that it might disappear from his grasp.

"It won't open!" he almost accused.

Laura wiped her hands on her clothes.

"Let me try," she said, picking up her sketch book and shoulder bag in readiness for a quick exit. Mr Millar reluctantly released the door handle and moved aside, but stayed close by watching Laura's every move. Slowly, slowly she walked towards the door and then at the last possible moment stretched out her hand. There was a sharp click and the door opened.

"Miss Trevillick," gasped Mr Millar, relief apparent in his voice. "My dear Miss Trevillick, I never doubted you for a moment."

So saying he brushed her aside and pushed his way through. Laura followed, shaking her head in disbelief at his rudeness. The light from the room which they had just vacated shone briefly on uneven, granite-like walls. Mr Millar, who had run on several paces, now stopped, stricken.

"Where are we?" he called. "Miss Trevillick – is this right?"

Before Laura could answer, the door, through which they had just come, closed – and they were plunged into darkness.

Laura stretched out her free hand. She moved slowly to the right and came into contact with what she assumed must be the wall that she had so briefly seen. It was cold, gritty and even slightly damp. Some way ahead of her she could hear Mr Millar breathing heavily. She heard him patting his hands over his clothing. Then there was a short pause, an excited exclamation and a noise as if something was being shaken for several seconds, then a 'click' and a sharp, clean light pierced the blackness.

"I always carry one of these – in case of emergencies – this is the first time though, that I've ever had to use it."

Mr Millar shone the torch around and its beam picked out rock all around them.

"If this is where you came from, Miss Trevillick," he declared apprehensively. "Then I fear I have made a terrible mistake….please tell me that we're both in the wrong place."

Laura was stunned. She'd somehow expected to get back into the house where everything had begun; that she'd then fly down the stairs, through the hall and out into the garden, back home in time for tea. But this! This was like a cave -   her heart thumped and she wondered if the door had hurled her back far into the beginning of time.

"Well?"

Laura wondered if Mr Millar had caused this strange occurrence – after all, the door would not open for him. Perhaps, when he had run through ahead of her, he had altered the mechanism in some disastrous way. She cleared her throat.

"I'm afraid I do not recognise this place at all Mr Millar. It doesn't resemble anything I've ever seen where I live."

Mr Millar brushed past her again and stretched out his hands to touch the rock where the door had been just a short while before.

"Extraordinary! Solid rock and no way back..." He started to laugh, a hideous and uncontrollable cacophony of sound. Normally, thought Laura, one might possibly expect to slap the face of a person suffering from this form of hysteria – she had seen this happen in any number of films – but she wasn't about to touch Mr Millar on any part of his body. Instead, she backed away, edging along the wall, carefully feeling with her hand, anxious to get as far away from this laughing hyena as possible. Then her hand felt - nothing! And her right foot dangled into air. She gasped and managed to pull herself back. Mr Millar's tortured laughter died away and the light of his torch swivelled in Laura's direction.

"What is it, Miss Trevillick? What have you found?"

He walked carefully over, surveying the walls and floor. When he reached Laura, the beam showed a large gap in the wall and a long, long drop close by her feet. Mr Millar gulped and took a deep breath.

"Forgive me, Miss Trevillick, I'm afraid I rather let myself down badly for a moment. This..er...This place was not at all what I was expecting. Let's see if I can be of some more practical help."

He shone the torch light along the floor level gap until the beam showed what appeared to be a solid, rock bridge across a three metre wide chasm. He lifted the torch so that its strong beam shone along what looked like a long, dark tunnel. Mr Millar stared ahead then he warned Laura that he was going to switch the torch off.

"Just keep very still while I do it though; we don't want you to plunge down a bottomless pit, do we?"

Laura shrank back into the wall, trying to ensure that she was as still as possible. When the light was switched off, the darkness cloaked itself around them like cold velvet.

"See there!" whispered Mr Millar. "In the distance."

Laura carefully forced her head round until she was able to stare ahead in relative comfort. Sure enough, in the distance there was a pinprick of light.

"Perhaps we'll be alright after all Miss Trevillick. Come over here then – carefully does it. Now then, as you are obviously the lighter of the two of us, perhaps you would be kind enough to cross the, ah, bridge first....just in case."

"What if it breaks half way along and I fall down the pit or whatever it is?"

"Alas, my dear Miss Trevillick, I will be marooned here for ever."

He held out his hand to help her on, but she drew back.

"I can manage myself, thank you," she said firmly.

"As you wish."

He held the torch steady and Laura concentrated on following the beam of light which played along the length of the bridge. Carefully she stepped on. It felt quite firm and she inched her way forward with short, mincing steps until she reached what she thought was the halfway point. There she suddenly came to a halt, aware of the inky black depth that lay beneath her. She felt her legs begin to tremble.

"What is it?" called Mr Millar impatiently. "You're fine. Keep going. Don't look down – that's what they say, isn't it? Keep staring straight ahead."

Laura clenched her fist. The shoulder bag felt as if it was about to slip off and she tightened her hold on it. She had no wish to lose that, especially now, after all that she had been through. Steadying her breathing, she lifted her head and concentrated on the small point of light some way in the distance and carefully placed one foot in front of the other and then the other and finally – she was across and standing on a solid floor once again. She breathed a huge sigh of relief and gave a 'whoop' which set echoes clattering around her ears, then turned to watch Mr Millar.

"Right then," she called. "Your turn."

The light from across the other side of the bridge wavered and pointed downwards. She heard Mr Millar shuffling forward. Then he stopped. Laura waited patiently, for about ten seconds. After that she became aware that absolutely nothing was happening.

"Mr Millar is everything alright."

She heard him swallow, but other than that there was no reply.

"Mr Millar, come on, I'm getting cold standing here waiting for you."

At last he found his voice, which when Laura heard it was quivery and unsteady.

"You go on then. I'll wait here."

"What?"

"Go on! I will be fine....here."

"Mr Millar what is the matter?"

There was another yawning gap of silence and then Laura heard what she was sure was a whimpering sound.

"Mr Millar? Is that you?"

"I'm.....I'm here.....Miss Trevillick....but.....I'm .....frigh....frightened..."

Laura stepped back in amazement. Then she pulled herself together.

"I don't understand. What are you frightened of?"

Again there was a pause, but this time not for so long.

"I........suppose...it's...sort...of......elementary. Suddenly....I'm...outside....in the ...dark....there's no Computer.........to...........guide......................me and....quite....unfamiliarly...I," Mr Millar gulped noisily. "I feel a terrible fear. It's being outside ...BCS...you...see..."

Laura didn't want to, but she couldn't help feeling sympathy for the man.

"But Mr Millar, you've been outside BCS before, you told me so yourself."

"Yes, but that was quite different – I could get back. Here, though, there's no going back and I'm...I'm...homesick."

Laura, whose sympathy dried up rapidly, couldn't stand any more of this. She walked briskly across the bridge, took the torch from Mr Millar's shaking hand, and then grasped that hand in her own, firmly.

"Ready, Mr Millar? Just follow me and we'll be across in no time. Ready?"

"Yes, Miss Trevillick, thank you, I'll be fine now. Thank you."

Laura retraced her steps with much greater confidence now and in no time at all, just as she'd said, she and Mr Millar were across the bridge. Thankfully she released the sticky hand.

"There, we're safe again. Shall we go on?"

And without waiting for a reply she boldly went, as she later discovered, where no twelve year old child had gone before.

Chapter 21

They walked on, carefully, keeping the small point of light in view. Every few metres Mr Millar would pause, switch off the torch and allow the darkness to descend; but always, the light ahead shone, and, gradually, grew more distinct. Mr Millar would give the torch a vigorous shake and switch it on again and the strong light would pierce the blackness once again.

"How long does the torch stay charged?" asked Laura at one point.

"Several hours – I don't even have to shake it really; that's just an unnecessary habit."

From time to time he would cast the bright light over their surroundings and they would gaze at the walls almost suspiciously. To Laura it appeared to be part of an old mining tunnel, though there was no sign now of any supporting timbers. The thought of tons of granite above her head made Laura feel distinctly uncomfortable and she kept gazing upwards to make sure that the roof wasn't moving. Having also studied mining at her primary school some years earlier, she was surprised at how dry the walls and floor appeared.

They had now been walking for some time and Laura was beginning to tire – so was Mr Millar, for that matter, to judge from the way he was walking, dragging his feet rather than lifting each step eagerly. At last he stopped.

"Forgive me Miss Trevillick," he rasped. "I must rest for a moment....I am not really used to such seemingly purposeless activity."

He leaned back against a wall and allowed his body to slowly sink down into a crouch position. Laura, too, was glad to stop and rest, but barely had she sat down on the opposite side of the tunnel when she heard a loud noise; it was coming from the direction in which they were travelling. Something was approaching them at a slow but steady rate of speed. Mr Millar switched off his torch and they both saw what appeared to be headlights approaching. The truck, or so it appeared, continued to advance, and they stood and pressed themselves against the walls to avoid being crushed. The truck was pushing a trailer in which rested a coffin, at least that's what it looked like to Laura. The truck stopped, steam belching from a chimney pot. Two elderly gentlemen were on board, one steering the truck and the other stoking the boiler with fuel.

"What have we here, Mr Shipley?" called the driver.

Mr Shipley looked up from his stoking and stared first at Laura and then at Mr Millar.

"Nobody that I know, Mr Symons, in fact, by rights nobody should even be here!"

Laura stared at the two men. They were definitely quite aged – their faces were lined with wrinkles and laughter lines, but she had no idea just how old they might be. The thought fleetingly crossed her mind that these might be 'knockers', fairy miners who haunted old mine workings, but she dismissed the idea as foolish and fanciful.

116

"I am Mr Millar, head of security at Bodmin City State, and this is Miss Trevillick."

"Hop in then," said Mr Symons, not unkindly. "Be quick though, we have a job to complete here."

Mr Millar clambered in, glad to have another mode of transport, while Laura was helped into the truck by Mr Shipley. The vehicle moved off again, back towards the bridge. It was a slow and steady pace, and Laura was reminded of the traction engines she had seen on special occasions in Cornwall. The two elderly gentlemen went about their business calmly, intent upon their mission, whatever it was, only occasionally glancing at the two unexpected travellers. In a short time they reached the chasm and the trailer was carefully manoeuvred on to the bridge. Mr Symons pulled a lever and the side of the trailer came down.

"We consign thee to the depths," said Mr Symons authoritatively. "May you rest in eternal peace." He pulled another lever and the coffin was shunted across the trailer by a piston; it teetered for a moment on the edge, and then it was over the side, plunging down into the chasm. The piston returned to its original position as did the side of the trailer; the engine was put into reverse and the truck shunted its way back, Mr Symons steering carefully and capably. On the way back, once they were moving steadily, he spoke to Laura.

"You're a fine looking maid, but this is no place for a young girl. How old are you?"

"I'm twelve," Laura paused for a moment, then added "Or possibly thirteen by now."

Mr Symons whistled.

"Twelve years old – why, you're not much more than a baby!"

Laura was not pleased to find herself being described as a baby. She considered herself an intelligent girl; and what's more, she felt that in the last few days in BCS she had aged considerably.

"If it's not too impolite to ask," she said. "How old are you?"

Mr Symons scratched his head.

"That's a tricky one. Now Mr Banham, he's the chap we just said farewell to, well, he was 268, so if I can just do a quick calculation in my head," he paused for a moment while Laura's thoughts whirled in astonishment. "Yes," he continued. "I reckon I must be 142 years of age. Course, there's a lot much younger than me and Mr Shipley; and a fair few that are a good bit older!"

He was silent after that nougat of information while he steered around a bend. This was where the light, which Laura and Mr Millar had seen earlier, had been coming from, and as the truck moved round the curve in the tunnel, they came into a much larger cave which looked something like a goods yard. The truck was checked in to a depot where several other similar trucks were parked. In attendance, cleaning, polishing and generally making themselves useful, was a variety of other people – all in the senior age bracket. They stared at the newcomers in open astonishment, while Laura and Mr Millar stared back, equally perplexed.

"Now then, while Mr Shipley banks down the boiler, I'll take you along to reception which is a fair walk from here. Most people arrive in the normal manner and don't usually appear out of nowhere."

Mr Symons then began to usher them out of the truck, but as he did so Mr Millar held up his hand.

118

"Just where, exactly, is 'here'?" he asked.

"Why, I thought you would have known that, being a security man and seeing as how you came to be walking along a normally deserted tunnel, happy as you please."

"I am not particularly 'happy'," snapped Mr Millar. "All I require is a straightforward answer to a straight forward question."

Mr Symons rubbed his chin.

"Hmm, yes. Forgive me, but, what question was that?"

Mr Millar looked, for a moment, as if he was going to explode. Laura intervened quickly.

"Can you just tell us where we are," she asked politely. "What do you call this place?"

"Now why didn't he say that right off?"

Mr Millar breathed in very deeply but managed to keep a tight rein on his temper, though the effort made his face red and a large vein to pulse on his forehead.

"I think that's what Mr Millar meant," said Laura.

"Well, you'll find out soon enough, I suppose, though I'm not surprised you're so mystified. So was everyone else when we first arrived."

"Arrived from where?" asked Laura.

"Why from BCS of course, where else?"

Mr Millar stopped in his tracks. For a moment it looked as if he would faint such was the strange expression on his face.

"Here," said Mr Symons, pulling on Mr Millar's arm. "You'd better sit down young feller. I'm sorry, I thought, being the security officer for BCS you might have known about us and been sent to investigate."

Mr Millar allowed himself to be seated on a stool which Mr Symons had kindly produced from a nearby truck, and bending forward rested his head on his hands. Laura was still puzzled, though she felt now that she was on the verge of understanding.

"But, how do you get here?" she asked.

"You really don't know?"

Laura shook her head.

"Well now, that's a turn up. I'm not sure I'm supposed to tell you. It's obviously still a secret up in BCS."

Mr Millar lifted his head.

"Up in BCS?"

"That's right." Mr Symons looked upwards. "Somewhere up there, above the tons of granite, is BCS – the first adventure! Down here, the rest of your life!"

"But how do you get here?" Laura repeated, beginning to understand Mr Millar's frustration.

Mr Symons looked round, then he bent down and whispered in Laura's ear "Have you ever heard of the Euthanasia Chute?"

Laura gasped.

"Yes," she said. "I once fell down it myself."

Now it was Mr Symons' turn to be surprised.

"You fell down it! Well I never! How on earth did that happen?"

Mr Millar jumped to his feet, anxious now to intervene.

"Never mind that," he said dismissively. "Are you telling me that you came here, to this – this place, via the Euthanasia Chute?"

Mr Symons grinned and nodded.

"That's right. Of course, I'm used to the idea now. I'm well past the shock I had when I first arrived – after all, when you're floating down that chute you're preparing yourself for death. That's why we have a proper reception committee now. We can deal with all those people who think they've entered some sort of 'after-life'" He chuckled to himself. "It's a really great feeling when you realise you're still alive with at least another hundred years ahead of you. Anyway, that's all by the by, so come on now, I'll take you to reception where I'm sure all the rest of your questions will be answered."

So saying he took Laura's hand and proceeded to lead them through Bodmin City State's underworld kingdom.

Chapter 22

Laura was delighted. She had been so shocked and saddened at the thought of people having to fling themselves into the Euthanasia Chute, hurtling, apparently, to their deaths, that to now, suddenly discover that it was merely a transition from one, rather authoritarian regime to a world where the life expectancy was well in excess of the norm, was just such a wonderful revelation. She felt as if a huge and heavy cloud of sorrow had simply and completely vanished. She also wondered what Mr Millar thought. He had, after all, been hoping to step through the door and back into the 21st Century...; and here he was, as far as she could tell, still firmly trapped in his own time, though in a totally different environment. Laura looked back at him as he followed, but there was nothing on his face to indicate just how he felt about the situation, other than a clear determination to get to 'reception' in order to obtain more answers. Laura tried to imagine what life in this 'underworld' was really like and whether Mr Millar would be happy to remain here... and if the present inhabitants would be happy to receive him – or her for that matter. There might, after all, be a special rule that stated that only those over the age of 60 could live her. What, in that case, would happen to Mr Millar and her? Would they be expelled or worse, imprisoned until they reached the 'magic' age? Laura tried to put a stop to these thoughts. 'Why worry about things over which you have no control,' she tried to assure herself.

As they walked through first one tunnel and then another, they passed groups of people engaged in different activities. Some were painting the tunnel walls in bright colours and Laura's fingers itched to add her own decoration. Others were in the process of making tools of various kinds. In one enormous area they passed by a huge field of what looked like cultivated mushrooms, with large groups of workers lovingly tending or harvesting these interesting fungi. Eventually they were taken into a refectory where men and women sat eating together. Mr Symons asked if they were hungry and Laura realised just how famished she was.

"Do you have supplies of food bars then?" she asked.

Mr Symons laughed uproariously.

"That awful stuff! No, what you get down here is 'proper job' food. You'll see."

He led them to a vacant table where the two new arrivals sat down, while he went to a large circular canteen area. The noisy hubbub of the refectory became much less as many pairs of eyes turned towards them. Laura, in particular, came in for much scrutiny. However, like the citizens of BCS, these also were too polite to approach them directly. Laura concentrated on watching Mr Symons collect a tray and then proceed to fill it with several items. When he returned with the laden tray Mr Millar eyed everything with great suspicion, but to Laura some of the things on the tray seemed almost familiar. There was a teapot, with cups, some hot round objects that looked amazingly like burgers and in a large bowl there were what could only be 'chips'!

"There now," said Mr Symons. "Help yourselves. There's a special tea that we make ourselves in the pot; these are mushroom fritters with crispies in the bowl, and this is our own cakebread. Everything made from home grown ingredients. Go on then, get stuck in, I don't suppose they'll mind waiting a bit longer in reception."

Laura sniffed. The steaming hot food smelled good – very good. She helped herself to a fritter and some crispies/chips. Carefully she used the spoon and fork provided to eat the food.

"Mmm!" she enthused. "That is so delicious."

"Here try some tea, it's supposed to be very good for you." Mr Symons poured some of the brew into a cup. Mr Millar watched enviously. Clearly he felt somewhat inhibited by the sight of what appeared to be totally alien food – especially since it was 'home grown' rather than produced by Computer. After a moment though, he began to help himself. He had no idea about what to do with the spoon and fork so just used his fingers. Mr Symons watched with an amused expression on his face.

"Now that's very interesting," he declared. "Here's this young lady, who's a mere wisp of a thing and yet she clearly knows how to handle the utensils, while you, sir, are behaving in just the same way as our normal newcomers."

Mr Millar was, by now, chomping on his food with a look of astonishment on his face. For a moment he was unable to reply as he struggled to swallow all that he had in his mouth. He licked his fingers appreciatively.

"To answer your observation, I would advise you that Miss Trevillick is not, nor ever has been, a citizen of BCS. She is a very rare visitor."

So saying, he resumed his meal.

Laura looked around her while he was eating. She was amazed at how light everything appeared. She thought it would be a world of semi-darkness, but the beams of light were everywhere.

"How come it's so bright here Mr Symons?" she asked.

Mr Symons looked round.

"You're right, you know; it is bright. To tell you the truth, I've been here so long that I've just got used to it – take it for granted. The fact is much of the light and power that we have down here is the unused residue from up there." He pointed a finger straight above his head. "There are so many solar panels on the surface constantly absorbing energy that if a lot of it didn't come down here, then there'd probably be an overload in the system!"

"So all your heat and light comes from BCS?"

"Quite a lot of it," He rubbed his chin thoughtfully. "I can't say too much, seeing as how you've not been through registration yet, but I will say that even if we didn't have this generous facility we'd still be far from living in the stone age. Mind you, it doesn't come as easy as it does up there. We have to grow or manufacture and process our own food supplies; everything we use – tools, apparatus, living accommodation – all this has to be made, serviced and maintained. 'Computer' doesn't lend a hand like up there. Luckily, we've got a very willing, as well as very able workforce."

By now Mr Millar had finished his feast and the tray was returned, washed, dried and then they continued on their way to the reception. As they were walking Mr Symons drew Laura to his side and whispered "Tell me, Miss Trevillick, and forgive me if I seem nosy, but what did your friend mean when he said that you're a 'very rare visitor'?"

Laura didn't quite know how to answer. What could she say – that she'd slipped inside a house in the year 2009 and then, when she left the house found herself in the same place, only a thousand years later? Or how absurd it would sound if she confessed to being an unwilling time traveller? If, indeed, that's what she was. She tried to be diplomatic.

"It's difficult for me to describe what happened. All I can say is that I don't normally live at BCS."

Mr Symons nodded his head. "Fair enough," he said. "I shouldn't have been prying anyway. Our existence down here must seem very odd to you, come to think of it. I've no idea what your Mr Millar makes of it!"

"He's not my Mr Millar!" Laura was shocked that she was seen as being so closely linked to the security man. "Nor is he my 'friend' – he just attached himself to me."

Mr Symons gave Mr Millar a questioning look but made no further comment. They continued the rest of the walk in silence. Mr Symons led them through various passages and tunnels until at last, they reached the reception area.

Laura hadn't been quite sure what to expect, but in the event, she was taken by complete surprise at the sight of a vast lake in the centre of a huge cavern, the ceiling of which seemed as tall as a cathedral. Boats were crossing from one side of the lake to the other. One boat appeared to be a fishing vessel. Even Mr Millar's eyes bulged again as he surveyed the scene. Mr Symons pointed up to the top of the cavern where a structure had been built – similar, thought Laura, to an aircraft's escape slide.

"In the early days," said Mr Symons. "When the first people fell down the Euthanasia Chute, they fell straight into this lovely fresh water lake – it was a bit tragic because some of them drowned, not being that used to water. But after a generation or so, the groups organised themselves better and gradually the infrastructure for our civilisation was developed down here. That contraption you see there gives new arrivals a really nice soft landing and they slide down to dry land without getting a bit wet, straight to the reception area – which is where I am now going to take you; if you'll just follow me."

He walked to the edge of the lake where a punt-like boat was tied. A tall man with long white hair was sitting on board.

"Ah Harry," called Mr Symons. "Two passengers, new arrivals, for reception, if you please."

Harry stared at Laura and Mr Millar.

"Where did they come from?" he asked, looking perplexed.

"Never mind that now, I'll tell you later. Just take us across, will you, there's a good chap."

Without waiting for a response, Mr Symons stepped into the boat and indicated to Laura that she should follow him. He helped her on board and she made her way to a seat. Mr Millar, who had had no experience of any sort of boat, clambered on board very unsteadily and would have fallen into the water had not Harry caught hold of him.

"Here, here, steady on young feller," he said. "Or you'll have us all overboard if you're not careful." Instead of thanking him, Mr Millar just glared at Harry. Mr Symons leaned across and undid the rope and when all the passengers were seated – though Mr Millar himself looked distinctly uncomfortable, grasping the board on which he was perched, very tightly – Harry, their boatman, used a long pole to punt the boat round the edge of the lake.

"Why don't we go straight across?" asked Laura.

Mr Symons chuckled. "If we did that, Harry would have to abandon his pole and get oars out. It's far too deep to punt anywhere other than round the edge. Just relax and enjoy the ride."

With a groan, and still gripping his seat as if his life depended on it, Mr Millar closed his eyes, gritted his teeth and looked anything but relaxed.

Chapter 23

Laura looked at her surroundings. The water was jet black, but with lights dotted around the lake, the surface sparkled as if filled with stars. She could see now that the distance across the lake was enormous. Harry's punting was faultless and as they gently rounded the edge of the lake she could see that they were approaching the point at which the slide met the shore. Here there was, extraordinarily, a large tent.

"That's the reception area," said Mr Symons. "Where our new arrivals are met and welcomed. We had our last batch only a week or so ago."

Laura caught her breath.

"Was there a lady called Vera and a man called David in that group?"

"I'm sorry, I've no idea. I don't normally meet the new arrivals – that's why seeing you and Mr Millar was such a surprise for me. If you want to locate particular people you'll have to speak to Miss Dunn, she's the senior in charge – she'll have a record of all the latest people to get here safely. Now hold tight, we're here now – be ready to disembark."

The punt edged towards a small jetty and Harry skipped nimbly off the punt and in a swift and practised movement secured the boat with the landing rope. Mr Symons got off next and helped Laura, who stepped onto the jetty, still continuing to take in all the strange new sights around her. Mr Millar crawled off rather unsteadily by himself and found his legs wobbled as he stood.

"Thanks Harry." Mr Symons shook the boatman's hand. Laura did the same, much to Harry's surprise and delight. Mr Millar was still finding his land legs, so Harry clapped him on the shoulder which caused Mr Millar to stagger in an even more ungainly fashion.

"Now, follow me you two and I'll take you in to meet Miss Dunn – as I said, she's the senior who signs in all the new arrivals. She will allocate you appropriate accommodation and eventually you'll be assigned to jobs suited to your skill and abilities."

Mr Symons scratched his chin again, while looking first at Laura and then at Mr Millar. "At least, that's what usually happens. You two might be a bit more difficult, or that is to say, less easy to deal with. Yes, that's it, less easy..."

He went into the reception tent and Laura and Mr Millar followed. Inside there were tables and chairs and at the far end of the tent a much larger and longer table behind which sat a formidable looking woman. The floor they crossed was covered with amber coloured, woven matting which was pleasant to walk on. As they neared the table Mr Symons raised his cap.

"Greetings to you Miss Dunn," he said politely.

"And to you Mr Symons," replied the woman. "You are a long way from your precious steam locomotives. This must be a very important assignment to drag you away from them."

Mr Symons, who wasn't too sure whether he was being reprimanded or praised, quickly ushered Laura and Mr Millar forward.

"I've found two unexpected arrivals Miss Dunn, in the consignment corridor; they were, er, wandering along down there, just as I was delivering old Mr Banham to his final resting place."

Miss Dunn stared at the 'unexpected arrivals' with a clear and penetrating gaze. She had a strong featured, intelligent face with a mass of deep brown curls that suited her very well. Laura knew she must be over 60 years old but, other than that, she had no clue whatsoever as to her actual age.

Miss Dunn nodded and motioned for Laura and Mr Millar to sit down. Her gaze lingered briefly over Mr Millar, but she devoted considerable time to staring at Laura. Mr Millar, not used to being ignored, cleared his throat. Miss Dunn's eyes remained fixed on Laura but she held up a large, slim hand. "All in good time, sir," she said. "All in good time. Come closer young lady."

Laura got to her feet and walked up to Miss Dunn.

"This is Miss Trevillick," said Mr Symons, trying hard to be useful.

"Thank you, Mr Symons. I can deal with these newcomers now. You have your normal duties to attend to, do you not?"

Mr Symons rubbed his chin, but wisely kept quiet. He waved goodbye, a little reluctantly, Laura thought, and returned the way he had come, glancing back every now and again. "Goodbye Mr Symons," called Laura. "Thanks for the food!" He waved again, and with a big grin climbed back into the waiting punt.

Miss Dunn then asked Laura for her full name and age, the details of which she carefully wrote into a large ledger using a quill pen and ink. Mr Millar stared at these implements in amazement. Laura realised that such things must look like ancient museum pieces to his technologically influenced way of life.

"You present me with quite a dilemma, Laura – May I call you that? It seems inappropriate for me to refer to you as Miss Trevillick."

"Of course," said Laura. "I much prefer that myself."

At that point Mr Millar interrupted. "And how much longer do I have to wait here before I am attended to?"

"And you are?"

"I am Mr Bartholomew Millar, former head of security in Bodmin City State – and I will, of course, expect due deference to be paid to someone of my status."

Miss Dunn allowed a brief, but thin-lipped, smile to flit across her face.

"You will receive the same respect that all our other newcomers receive. Once a person gets here, whatever their previous status, he or she is considered as being equal to all those who have registered or are yet to be registered. Naturally, we try to fit a person's abilities to suit the tasks required in this world; but you must appreciate, Mr Millar, that our needs here are entirely different to those of BCS. As a new entrant you will be given a number of tasks – including gardening," Miss Dunn ignored the look of disgust on Mr Millar's face. "– farming, mechanics, fishing and so on. Your first year mentor will make an assessment of your abilities and report to the central committee. That report will help us to decide your future."

Mr Millar opened his mouth as if to protest, but Miss Dunn continued forcefully.

"What you must remember also Mr Millar is that life expectancy here is considerably longer than you could ever have imagined. During the course of their lifetimes many of our citizens undertake several different careers, so you may rest assured that whatever qualities you possess will be put to good use. Now what is your age please?"

Mr Millar's eyes flickered towards Laura. He looked down at his feet.

"You do know how old you are Mr Millar?"

Mr Millar cleared his throat.

"I'm…." he mumbled inaudibly.

"Please speak up Mr Millar."

"59!"

Miss Dunn stared hard at the man in front of her.

"So. You were afraid to go down the Euthanasia Chute. How interesting."

Mr Millar went very red.

"I was not afraid," he shouted. "I just felt I was destined for better things."

"Ah, a man of destiny. Very well, I'm sure that we will be able to find you something suitable."

She picked up a hand bell on her desk and rang it. A kind faced woman with a warm smile stepped forward. She was dressed in an amber coloured boiler suit.

"Daphne here will show you around Mr Millar. By the time you have acquainted yourself with our facilities and returned here I will have more idea of what you can be usefully allowed to do."

Daphne took hold of Mr Millar's hand.

"Really," he began. "I am not a child, I…"

"Oh do stop that fussing sir," said Daphne. "And come along with me. Every body enjoys the tour." So saying she pulled a still-protesting Mr Millar along behind her.

"We usually have no problems," said Miss Dunn. "Normally the new arrivals are so shocked to find that they're still alive that they allow themselves to be led like small domestic animals. Mr Millar, however, does not look as though he's going to be quite so amenable."

"I don't think he was very happy in BCS," said Laura.

"Quite. So, tell me, how is it that you both appeared here together in a place not ever known for new arrivals?"

Laura told Miss Dunn as much as she thought reasonable, though when she mentioned the doorway into the tunnel, she couldn't help noticing Miss Dunn's quizzically raised eyebrows. Laura also could not bring herself to describe Mr Millar's deadly use of weapons, thinking that in the circumstances in which he now found himself, it was entirely possible that he could become a more caring member of this society. She did say, however, that she felt that he had become slightly unbalanced and expressed the hope that 'Daphne' would be able to look after herself.

Miss Dunn smiled.

"You need have no worries about that. All our mentors are specially trained. No, I'm not concerned about Daphne or the rather pompous Bartholomew Millar. What most concerns me at this moment is what we do with a twelve year old girl who is certainly not likely to fit in to this world or who, I suspect, was not naturally native to Bodmin City State."

She stared at Laura who felt extremely uncomfortable, believing that all the layers of subterfuge that she'd built around herself were being slowly and efficiently peeled away.

"I can draw," she said hastily, handing over her sketch book. "And I don't mind old people."

Miss Dunn smiled and took the book, glancing through it at first and then studying it more intently.

"You do have a formidable talent, and I am so pleased to hear that you are able to put up with 'old' people...." Laura had the good grace to blush. "....especially as the age range down here goes from 60 up to as much as 260; I suppose Mr Symons told you that our late Mr Banham reached 268 years of age?"

Laura nodded. "That's so amazing. How is it possible for people to live so long here?"

"Oh I blame Computer."

"Computer?" Laura looked around. She hadn't seen any evidence of Computer anywhere – there were certainly no screens visible.

"Don't worry. Computer has no direct influence in these parts. What I meant was that, thanks to Computer's genetic manipulation, every person who makes it down here is in perfect health. None of us is subject to any of the diseases to which elderly people may once have been subject. Which means that our population is growing, which thus means that we all have to work hard to maintain food supplies, clothes manufacturing, mechanical engineering and so on. Every single person has to put back into our society what he or she gets out of it. Up there..." she pointed, "People have a pretty boring, but nevertheless, easy life. All our newcomers have to deal with the shock of coming to terms with a completely new way of life. This brings me on to you."

Laura looked up, rather guiltily.

"Me?"

"I don't think you're quite as innocent as you look. Nor, if my memory serves me correctly, do you have the look of any of the children I have ever known in BCS. Nor do I particularly believe parts of your, otherwise, very entertaining story."

Laura blushed again. Miss Dunn smiled.

"Don't worry – I still think you're going to be less troublesome than Mr Millar. Having said that, I'm going to show you round myself – not because I don't trust you, but because I'm pleased to meet someone who is so different – someone who is quite clearly not old!"

Chapter 24

Miss Dunn took Laura on what amounted to a 'Grand Tour'. With the aid of various 'taxis', some of which were steam driven and some of which were like bicycle-powered rickshaws, they made good progress and Laura was constantly astonished by the amount of space available, the equipment in use and by the ways in which different areas were organised.

"We owe a great debt to the first survivors," said Miss Dunn. "They had the wisdom to explore this environment and to begin to appraise all that was available to them."

"But that must have taken ages!" said Laura.

"Oh yes, of course, but when they realised that they had air to breathe and water to drink, they gradually found that the desire to survive was very strong. Besides which, much of the infrastructure that you see here was already established."

Laura looked around her immediate vicinity.

"You mean the machines and tunnels were already here?"

"That's right; and even stocks of food. It seems, from very old records that we've discovered, that with the fear of nuclear war imminent, various underground establishments like this were constructed, and much later, above these facilities and totally independent of them, the first city states were built – in readiness for the destruction of the ozone layer and the huge rise in the level of the seas and oceans."

"How many of these city states were built?"

"Not nearly enough. Lack of time and a lack of resources meant that only a few suitable areas in Britain were found, some more in the United States, a few in Europe, one or two in Australia I believe, one in Israel and one in South Africa."

"And that's it; that's all that remains of the human race?"

"As far as we know."

Laura shuddered. Humanity forced to live below ground and then, here and possibly elsewhere, even further below that level – never to venture out except in protective suits; it was like living on a totally different planet.

"Will the ozone layer ever repair itself?" she asked hopefully.

Miss Dunn was silent for a moment. Her reply was cautious.

"I've only ever lived underground, so I haven't the same feelings for the outside as you have. Nevertheless from what I can recall, scientists in the city states continued to monitor the atmosphere and the ozone layer. It might have been fine if there had been a few areas of the layer left intact....that way there might have been a hope of some form of regeneration to take place at some time in the future. Unfortunately, when I was in BCS, no such regeneration was ever discovered. Besides which, so many areas of the Earth's surface were covered by water that living above ground would have been impractical anyway. But please, don't worry yourself Laura. As you go round you will only meet happy and contented people."

"I won't be happy, though, until I get back to my own family," said Laura.

Miss Dunn looked down at the child who walked beside her.

"So you really are from a different time zone altogether."

Laura nodded. "How did you know?"

"We never ever get children down here and the only experiences I have of them is from a, thankfully, brief visit in BCS to a school unit. Family life, unlike your obvious heart-felt statement, was something that was never encouraged – in fact, I suspect it was bred out of us by Computer. So, to meet someone like you, desperate to get back to her own family, is to encounter a person who is neither of this time nor of this place."

Laura relaxed at last. She hadn't wished to be in this underground world under false pretences

"Thanks," she said. "You must be a very wise person."

Miss Dunn smiled rather wistfully.

"Just because I know a few facts doesn't make me wise at all. I know what I know about this time and this place, but I haven't the faintest notion about your life – nor," she added just as Laura was about to interrupt, "do I wish to know. I do not want my life turned upside down by a twelve year old from Computer knows when. So I shall just accept you as a visitor who may, or may not, be with us for the foreseeable future. That way, if you do one day disappear, I shall not be in the least bit disappointed."

Seeing Laura's lower lip beginning to quiver, Miss Dunn moved on quickly to change the subject.

"Well, come along then, we still have lots to do," and without a trace of self-consciousness she took Laura's hand and announced "and there's also the farm, which I'm sure you'll enjoy."

The 'farm' was not, as Laura had expected, the giant mushroom field, but much, much more. There were several caverns of wheat fields; two rice 'paddies' and amazingly a herd of dairy cows.

"How on earth did you get these down here?" asked an incredulous Laura.

"Ah," said Miss Dunn, quite proudly. "As I said, the infrastructure was already in place, complete with nuclear generators, power and fuel together with the means to rear animals from frozen embryos – which is where we get our herd of Jersey cows. We also have sheep and goats. All these animals give us supplies of milk and cheese products as well as wool and leather for our clothes industry. Even so, with our ageing and increasing population it is not always easy to keep up with demand."

While Laura had been on her tour she'd noticed the enormous number of labourers working in the fields, hence her next question: "Do the people who work get paid?"

"Paid?" said Miss Dunn, as if Laura had mentioned a rude word. "Do you mean with money?"

"Yes."

Miss Dunn shook her head in disbelief.

"My dear girl, we have had no use for money, either down here or up there. Money was only in use because of international trade. In confined organisations such as ours we have no use for money,. Everyone has to work, or rather I should say everyone wants to work in order to help the community to thrive. Nor, incidentally, do we spend hours counting up what this person or that person does. It's part of our breeding program again I suppose; we all have something called the 'work ethic'. We are all happy in our work and because of our continuing good health, we work until we die. In addition, we have a variety of different jobs in our new lifetimes. While a person is down here he or she can have several different and equally worthwhile careers. I haven't always worked in reception, for example; before then I'd worked on the farm; in one of the canteens; I've even been a cobbler. The opportunities here are marvellous. If you remain with us you will have a vigorous and entertaining life."

Laura's head sank at the thought of remaining for the rest of her life in an underground city.

"Don't look so miserable," said Miss Dunn. "We won't put you to work just yet; you'll have plenty of time to become acclimatised," she paused. "Unless, that is, you know of a way back?"

Laura shook her head.

"We got here by chance, I don't know how and I've no reason to suppose that I'll ever get back home."

At this point the thought of her own home in the soft Cornish countryside, with her parents, their two cats, the parrot and her white floppy-eared rabbits brought fresh tears to her eyes. Although she would not admit it, Miss Dunn was moved and reassuringly took Laura's hand again.

"We do not go in much for displays of kindness or tenderness – that excess of emotion has, over the centuries been yet another aspect of Computer's breeding regime – or perhaps it's just the way that we have evolved; even so, I can sense your unhappiness, even if I am unable to fully comprehend or empathise with it."

"So, are you never sad, or unhappy?"

"The truthful answer, which I'm sure you won't like to hear, is that, no, we do not experience such an over-abundance of emotions. When a member of our society dies, such as Mr Banham, we celebrate the achievements of that person; but we do not mourn. There seems no point in grieving."

They had by now, reached another cavern; this one was like a massive factory with row upon row of benches at which sat citizens of this underground society, busily stitching, sewing or knitting. Each individual was intent upon his or her activity. Laura had seen news clips showing thousands of dedicated Chinese workers, their eyes focussed on whatever it was they were doing. The scene that Laura was now witnessing reminded her of those Chinese workers and she didn't know whether to be impressed or alarmed. Even when they walked amongst the people working, their presence failed to distract them from their tasks, although Laura was aware of a few interested glances. Quite suddenly, however, a lady jumped up and greeted Laura warmly. Laura was startled at first and then realised that the woman shaking her hand vigorously was none other than Vera whom she had last 'met' in the Euthanasia Chute.

"It is Laura, isn't it?" said Vera. "So you made it after all?"

"Made it?" said Laura, still taken by surprise.

"Down the chute! We were so delighted to get here safely – it was such an amazing event, I'm still a bit dazed by it all."

Miss Dunn interrupted at that point.

"Have you two met before?"

Before Laura could speak, Vera answered for them both.

"Oh yes, we were all three of us, travelling down the Euthanasia Chute – though, of course, Laura here, having fallen in by accident, was rescued before she could be, well, you know; we all thought that, didn't we?"

She was still shaking Laura by her hand. As gently as possible, Laura withdrew her crushed fingers.

"Is David still with you?" she asked.

Vera's animated face changed.

"Oh no, we were assigned to different jobs; he's on an entirely, er, different sort of production line. We don't really get much opportunity to see each other much now. We're both very busy learning our new tasks. That's right isn't it Miss..er.."

"Miss Dunn! Now, get back to your work Vera, we mustn't halt production, must we?"

"No of course, that would never do; it's been very nice to see you again Laura."

She sat down and proceeded to get on with the task she had been doing – it seemed to be some sort of button making; there were, what appeared to be thousands of buttons passing by on a conveyor belt. Miss Dunn ushered Laura along, and, as if she could imagine Laura's thoughts, she added: "All new arrivals get to do rather trivial tasks when they first arrive – it gives them the chance to acclimatise."

As they passed through the rows of silent, absorbed workers, Laura wondered if she, too, would be given a 'trivial' task.

Chapter 25

As it happens, something far more dramatic was about to take place, which pushed the 'trivial task' idea way out of Laura's head.

Miss Dunn was just showing her the living quarters – rows and rows of single person cubicles on several layers of upper floors. Each room was identical in structure, with a platform bed built into the wall of the room, a table, one chair and a small cupboard. It seemed somewhat 'Spartan' to Laura, though in quite a number of the rooms the walls were decorated with paintings or drawings imprinted directly onto the surface of the walls.

"Some of our residents are quite artistic and like to express themselves," said Miss Dunn. "I'm sure you'd sympathise with that aspiration."

"Yes, but…"

"Go on Laura, but what?"

"Well, what other entertainments are there Miss Dunn. Not everybody paints. I've seen no books, no television…"

"Books, Laura! Television! I'm afraid we are far too busy for such things. Besides, the cubicles are generally for sleeping in only; therefore, they are rarely personalised."

Laura thought of her own bedroom – full of her own, highly personal touches, as well as clothes, drawing materials, two bookcases, a lap top for her school work, 'creative' toys and a rarely-made, but very comfortable bed. – I'm very lucky to have all that, - she thought to herself.

"But there is a central library," went on Miss Dunn, sensing, perhaps, Laura's disapproval. "Where book pods can be read if one has the time. If you'll follow me I will show you just…."

Before she was able to complete the sentence, there was a loud, booming noise which seemed to reverberate through the caverns.

"What ever is….." began Laura, but Miss Dunn cut her off by gripping her arm.

"The emergency alarm!" she said. "This has not had to be utilised in over two hundred years." She looked at young girl beside her with piercing eyes. "I hope it is just a coincidence that it is now heard shortly after your arrival. Quickly, you must follow me and try to keep up."

She sped off, almost at a run. Laura had no idea just how old Miss Dunn was, but she was seriously impressed by her level of fitness. Laura followed as best she could.

If Laura had expected some form of mass panic, then she was mildly disappointed. True, a number of people were rushing, like Miss Dunn, presumably to the source of the emergency, though how they knew where to run continued to remain a mystery. As they ran through various galleries Laura noticed that those who were working continued to do so, but, nevertheless, there was a vague sense of unease. Laura bent her head and looked up, wondering if, as she'd secretly feared all along, that water was seeping into the underground caves, but, to her relief, all seemed dry above.

Finally they arrived at the entrance to a cave system which had a large door installed with a sign that read 'Authorised Admittance Only'. Daphne, the mentor who had been assigned to Mr Millar, was standing outside, waiting in some distress, with the skin around her right eye turning a lurid shade of black, green and yellow. When she saw Miss Dunn she rushed over.

"Miss Dunn, Miss Dunn!" she called. "I couldn't help it – he saw the door and was heading towards it. I told him to keep hold of my hand, that the door was out of bounds to him; but he hit me! He actually hit me! I've never been struck before in my life – it was such a shock I can tell you…"

"Yes, yes, I'm sorry to hear that Daphne – but this is no time for hysteria. What exactly happened next?"

Daphne swallowed hard, glaring at Laura as if she was responsible, and, with an effort, controlled her trembling.

"That man, that friend of yours," she pointed accusingly at Laura who could only gasp open-mouthed at the unintentional insult. "He just rushed through the doors there shouting something like 'At last, I can escape!' I couldn't stop him – I was lying on the floor by then."

She burst into tears

"What's in there then?" asked Laura.

Miss Dunn looked sharply at her.

"Those are the doors to the self-perpetuating nuclear generators. They provide extra heat, light, hot water, power for our machines – without it our survival could be in jeopardy, and your Mr Millar has just run in there!"

Laura was getting angry herself.

147

"Well, if it's so precious and important, why isn't the door locked?"

There was a quick intake of breath from many of those around Laura – clearly, they were not impressed at this mere child's audacity.

"The doors are never locked," said Miss Dunn, her voice no longer quite so friendly. "Because everyone here can read and, moreover, everyone obeys the signs. Your friend, Mr Millar, is clearly a law unto himself."

"He's not a friend of mine!" Laura almost shouted. "He forced himself on me!"

"Whatever," said Miss Dunn. "Meanwhile, friend or not, Mr Millar could do untold damage in there. We must get him out before he causes harm."

"It's all in hand, Miss Dunn," said one of the men in a nearby group. "As soon as we discovered the entry, three reactor men donned their suits and went in. He can't get far – as soon as he entered through the second set of doors he would have been in mortal danger."

"Did they take a spare suit for him?"

The man nodded. "Not that that would do him any good," he added.

"Why is that?" asked Laura.

"Well miss," said the man, politely considering he seldom addressed 12 year old children. "These doors are really only used for routine maintenance. The two sets of lead lined doors keep out lethal radiation – but they're seldom opened anyway. Normal entrance is through special key operated airlocks on the other side of the nuclear complex. We should have fitted the same over this side, but in over two hundred years…"

"Yes, I know, there's never been any accidents."

"That's right. The problem is, of course, once you are inside you're subject to massive doses of random radiation, which is why we always wear the proper clothing. Without the appropriate suits, you're going to suffer irreversible damage."

"Exactly," interrupted Miss Dunn. "And Mr Millar's state of mind was obviously somewhat deranged. Computer knows what he will get up to when he starts suffering from the effects of the radiation. What I can't understand is why he entered a door which clearly said No Admittance." She turned to Laura. "Do you know why?"

"I'm afraid he had the idea that different doors could lead into a different way of life, an escape from imprisonment."

There was an array of bewildered looks from those standing around Laura. Miss Dunn's was positively disdainful. Suddenly there was a shout from someone on duty near the doors.

"Quiet, everyone, there's a message from inside. I'll put it on the loudspeakers.

"This is Morrison reporting from inside the reactor area. We've located the intruder. He's clearly been badly affected by the radiation; unfortunately we cannot get close enough to him to make a rescue. He has got hold of a metal bar and is threatening to cause damage to the machinery unless we send in the girl."

- Oh no – thought Laura. –Not again!-

Miss Dunn strode forward purposefully. She spoke into the intercom.

"This is Miss Dunn here. Is there any chance that he is capable of inflicting serious damage?"

"Normally we'd say no, but the man seems obsessed by an abnormal strength - it's impossible to predict what he will do."

"Try to stall him. Keep him talking – he cannot survive much longer."

Laura was amazed by Miss Dunn's coolness; she seemed to taking total charge of the situation. Miss Dunn looked at Laura.

"Don't look so worried," she said. "There is no way we would send in just anyone, least of all a child, into such a situation."

Laura breathed a sigh of relief, but this was short-lived. There was another shout from the intercom.

"Great Computer!"

"Morrison," said Miss Dunn. "What is it?"

"The man has run along the gantry above the reactor. He's very unsteady – we're going to see if we can reach him."

There was a pause. In the area outside there was complete silence while everyone waited. The seconds ticked by and the tension could be felt like a taut wire waiting to snap. Then the intercom burst into life with a shrill cry, followed by a siren.

"Morrison, what's happening now?"

"Miss Dunn," It was a different voice. "It's Gavin Hicks here. It's terrible – we were approaching the man when he suddenly raced towards Morrison. The two grappled and before I could reach to assist, they had both gone over ..... straight into the reactor. The dials are going crazy now....... It could blow at any moment."

A sudden hubbub – the noise of distraught voices, began to rise to panic level.

150

"Quiet everyone!" shouted Miss Dunn. "Quiet! There's an emergency team on its way to sort out the problem. Meanwhile, as a precaution, you will make your way to emergency area B in as orderly a fashion as possible. You will wait there until the all clear sounds. NOW GO!"

The crowd needed no further encouragement and immediately headed for the exits. Miss Dunn, Laura noticed, remained at the intercom, relaying instructions. Laura herself stayed where she was, not quite knowing what to do, and for some reason, feeling guilty at having been responsible for bringing Mr Millar into this hitherto safe and well ordered society. Miss Dunn saw her.

"What are you still doing here? You must get out at once – this whole area could blow. This is not a safe place … Run quickly – Please!"

Laura turned and headed for the tunnel down which she'd seen the crowd disappear. Entering the entrance, she looked back; Miss Dunn was still there …. What occurred next seemed to happen in slow motion. The doors, which had been the cause of all the trouble in the first place, suddenly burst out from their hinges, and flew through the air like cardboard cut-outs. A blast of air 'whooshed' out and Laura could see the shapes behind the glass shiver and tremble, as if affected by great heat. Miss Dunn was thrown back, but Laura was relieved to see she was crawling behind a radiation barrier. The blast of air hit a rock wall across the cavern and the resulting explosion caused a huge flurry of rocks to come flying towards Laura. Terrified, she ran as fast as she could along the tunnel. She had no idea where the others had gone – and up ahead there appeared to be several different branches. Which one was the correct exit? Meanwhile, Laura could hear a tremendous roaring behind her. Thinking now only about escaping but also worrying about how this catastrophe would affect this haven for the over 60s, Laura went straight for the central branch as pieces of rock were pelting her from all sides.

Inside this tunnel it was quite dark, but Laura could feel that she was moving upwards. To her dismay the sound was still following her, and was, if anything, getting louder. She ran as hard as she could, then, spotting a glow of light to her left from a small opening scrambled into it just as masses of dust and rock hurtled past. She barely had time to watch, however, as she now found herself sliding down, down, down. The noise from above began to fade but she was unable to halt her slide. What's more, her rate of descent was increasing. The sides were very smooth so Laura was unable to grip anything, and still she was descending! "Help!" she screamed. At that precise moment, out of the corner of her eye, she saw a door, a very familiar door. She stretched out her hand and just managed to grasp the handle. Her descent halted and for a moment she hung suspended. She felt her grip weakening and felt sure that she would be unable to hang on when there was a click and the door opened inwards and pulled her through. She released her hold, only to discover that she was no longer just sliding, but falling! "NO! Please, NOT AGAIN!"

Chapter 26

At some point Laura lost consciousness; either that, or the incredible rate of descent, as if she was falling through both time and space, took her breath away and caused her to black out. The extraordinary thing, as she later discovered, was that her sketchbook, which she had kept in the shoulder bag, remained with her throughout that desperate flight and its unwilling descents. What was equally extraordinary was that some time later Laura woke to find that she was no longer falling but lying in darkness, breathless, but nevertheless, reasonably comfortable, with no sensation of physical pain. Gradually she became aware of a light glowing, gently at first, but then becoming brighter. In the heart of the glow a human shape was forming.

The glow and the 'shape' stabilised; the human was clearly an older woman who stared in Laura's general direction, though not specifically at Laura.

"Laura, Laura," called the woman. "I'm hoping that you can see and hear me."

With a shock, Laura realised that there was a distinct familiarity about the woman…and with the realisation of who she was came a sense of wonder and relief.

"I hope you can hear me at any rate. We're not generally allowed to meet face to face – there's some physical law in existence which prevents this – but there might be other occasions as you get older and more experienced, when we can become aware of each other.

But I realise that this is your first experience of the house and what it can do. You must know by now, that I am an older version of you and that's why I know this adventure is your first – our first! I don't know how the house works – it's like some kind of portal to other times, alternative places." The older Laura smiled. "The worlds are your oysters! You have so much to look forward to – I almost envy you. But, a word of warning. Though the house is generally benevolent, it can also be quite mischievous, and you may find it does the unexpected. Deep breathing helps when that happens and knowledge that somehow or another I might be able to help if I am able. And if you're wondering about the portraits – I did them, while you were asleep. I think the House has affected me after all these years – perhaps it has made me just as cheeky. Oh dear, I can feel my time running out and I've still got so much to say to you. Thank you for all your drawings – your talent has given us a wonderful career….." Laura's older self began to fade, the glow growing paler. "God speed, my dear…and remember…expect the unex…."

The vision vanished.

"Wait," called Laura. "Don't go!"

Very faintly she thought she heard a "Good luck…." faintly echoing from somewhere a long way away. Laura's head dropped down, and she slept. The darkness around her maintained her protective barrier, until Laura's body had begun its recovery from recent traumas.

When Laura began to wake it was into a familiar room where the windows allowed the sunlight to forecast a new way ahead. She opened her eyes, took in the surroundings and sat up slowly. She wondered, for a moment, if it had all been a dream, but one look at the sketch book in her bag, convinced her that everything had happened as she remembered. Part of her was exhilarated at the thought of returning home, but there was also sadness at the way she had left, with chaos looming, Miss Dunn, as well as all the other citizens, both in the underworld and BCS itself, in mortal danger. Was this something she would have to get used to? As a catalyst for disaster? She did as her older mentor had advised – took some deep breaths. In her calm state of mind she accepted that events can occur over which her influence might be a factor – one way or another. In this last experience no one in BCS had foreseen the possibility of Mr Millar being homicidal, so how could any of it be her fault? There was also the wider issue of global warning and non stop wars. Could Laura, with her recent experience, now do something that could change the future? 'I know' – she thought – 'I'll ask Mum, she's always full of commonsense.'

With this in mind she got up briskly, marched to the door which opened smartly before she even held out her hand. Laura walked on to the landing – all seemed unchanged. She saw herself in the mirror and waved, and then put her hand down. The image in the mirror waved back.

"How do you do that?" asked Laura.

Without expecting an answer she continued on her way, down the double staircase, across the entrance hall to the main door of the house. Laura waited patiently. Nothing happened. She stretched out her hand and there was a click. The door slowly opened towards her. Laura held her breath, wondering what she would see. She stepped around the door, and was relieved to see the garden in sunshine, the flowers as bright as when she had last seen them a thousand years ago! And as she walked down the path, there on the gate, a bird was preening its wings, just as before, when she'd last looked back. Laura twirled round.

"Thank you House, for looking after me!"

Without waiting for, or expecting a reply she skipped up the path. Behind her, the door clicked back into position.

Laura began to run, full of pleasure at the prospect of seeing her mother….but already she had forgotten her older self's warning: "…it can be quite mischievous…"

If Laura had now been standing on the first floor of the house, looking from the window, instead of skipping, happy as a lark – she would have seen beyond the garden. She would see beyond the small village with its run-down houses, ill-kept streets and forlorn trees, to the old barn with its ancient, rusting farm implements and within, where a woman labours, not at her sculptures – but at the scrubbing, scrubbing, scrubbing of the vegetables that she has managed to forage for a meal. Oh yes, the woman undoubtedly looks like Laura's mother from this distance; but is it the same woman that Laura has known and loved all her young life? And is this the self-same village where Laura has been living these past few months?

Behind the skipping girl, the House feels some thing like remorse for its mischievous little trick. "Beware, young Laura," it breathes out in a sigh that is wafted through the air. "Beware…take care……your adventures don't stop here…We'll be seeing you again, soon."

Thanks to

My wife, Jacqueline, for her help and encouragement throughout the process of writing this book.

To Pat Lipert and Louise Garcia, two friends for reading through the manuscript and offering corrections and suggestions.

To Yselkla Hall, my first young reader, who said she really enjoyed this book. I hope there'll be plenty more for you to enjoy!

Also to Tony Cowell whose one year service as an agent I won in a 'Pitch Idol' competition in Falmouth, in October 2006. He didn't manage to sell 'Roboschool' (the projected book which I originally pitched) to any publisher but he did give me loads of encouragement to finish that novel and then to move on and write 'The Locked Door'.

Finally to all those tutors who have helped stimulate my creative writing efforts over the last few years.

The Author

Harvey Kurzfield was a primary school teacher for many years, most of them spent in Cornwall.
He retired from his last post in 2002 and has been writing in some form or another ever since!

159

Lightning Source UK Ltd.
Milton Keynes UK
24 March 2010

151814UK00002BA/1/P